BLUE RIDGE MURDER

CAROLYN LAROCHE

HOT TREE PUBLISHING

ALSO BY CAROLYN LAROCHE

MARSHALL BROTHERS

Murder on the Mountain

Blue Ridge Murder

DEFENDERS OF LOVE

Witness Protection

Homeland Security

Border Patrol

For information, contact the publisher, Hot Tree Publishing.

www.hottreepublishing.com

Editing: Hot Tree Editing

Cover Designer: BookSmith Design

Ebook: 978-1-922359-41-4

Paperback: 978-1-922359-42-1

For you, Dad.
You aren't with us anymore but
I hope I still make you proud.
Thank you for always
being supportive of my dreams.
I love you and I miss you.

CHAPTER ONE

"OH, NO YOU DON'T!" HE PULLED A U-TURN IN THE center of the road and doubled back to the corner. Little Jimmy was at it again.

The tires screeched as he slammed on the brakes and jumped out, barely remembering to put the vehicle in Park.

Little Jimmy shoved his hands in his pockets, taking several steps backward. "Yo, PoPo what you want now? Me and my boy here were just chitchattin'."

Evan glanced over at the boy, who still held a small plastic bag in his hand.

"Just chitchattin', huh?" Evan reached for the boy's hand, but the kid was way quicker than him. He took off down the street, shoving the baggie in his back pocket as he ran. Little Jimmy spun on his heel and ran in the opposite direction.

Evan took off after the kid, yelling over his shoulder to Little Jimmy, "I'll be by your place later with a warrant!"

Forgetting the well-known neighborhood dealer for the moment, Evan focused all his energy on running. That kid sure had some speed. As they came up to a busy intersection, the kid paused. Evan took advantage, throwing everything he had into running. The adrenaline kicked in then, his heart pounding in his chest, every muscle in his body straining to the max. In seconds, he tackled the kid to the ground.

The boy struggled hard. Sweat poured down Evan's face, running into his eyes, but he ignored it. He needed help, and he needed it fast.

He keyed the mic on his radio. "Suspect is resisting! Send backup! *Now!*"

The boy twisted his body, hard, nearly breaking free from Evan's hold on his wrists, but he held on.

"Ouch! You're hurting me!"

"Where's that backup?" Evan yelled into the mic. The boy seized the opportunity to jump to his feet

again. Evan managed to hold on to one of his arms, stumbling back to his feet.

"Two cars on the way." The dispatcher, usually all business, sounded annoyed.

"Stop resisting already, kid!" Detective Evan Marshall wrapped one arm across the kid's torso, holding him tight to his chest while he attempted to get one cuff on. "You're making this so much worse than it has to be!"

"I didn't do anything!" The teen boy bucked against Evan hard enough to knock the wind out of him, but he didn't let go.

"This will go so much better for you if you just. Stop. *Resisting*!" Gasping for breath, Evan managed to finally get one cuff on the kid.

"You can't arrest me! I didn't do anything wrong! I's just walkin' to school! Is it a crime to be fifteen now, man? Guilty while teenager?"

He hadn't noticed the heavy black boots the boy wore until one of them came slamming down on top of his foot, sending white-hot pain shooting through his entire body. Pretty sure he heard a couple of bones crack, Evan shoved as hard as he could, knocking the kid facedown into the grass. Before the boy could react, Evan threw himself on top of him, grabbing his other wrist and slapping the second cuff in place.

His foot throbbed inside his boot with the kind of pain that said there was no way he'd be walking away from this arrest, so he stayed right where he was, sitting on his suspect's legs and trying to ignore the pain.

"What's your name, kid?"

"Screw you," the boy growled.

"What is *wrong* with you?" Evan's patience had worn thin. He clicked his radio on again. "Suspect in custody but resisting. Where's that backup?"

"Get off me!" The kid tried to buck again but made no real impact this time against Evan's muscular frame still pinning him to the ground.

"Look, you're going to jail today. At first I might have given you a citation but since you just assaulted a police officer while resisting arrest—and I'm pretty sure you broke my foot in the process—you might as well accept the fact there's a cell with your name on it at juvie."

He got real quiet all of a sudden. Enough to worry Evan. A rowdy suspect that turned quiet was never, ever a good thing. "I can't go back there."

Evan shrugged, even though the kid couldn't see

him. "You shoulda thought of that *before* you stopped to see Little Jimmy over there."

The kid tried to roll to the side, but Evan's weight held him firmly in place. "I don't know no Little Jimmy. And I didn't buy no pot."

Evan stuck his hand in the back pocket of the jeans the kid wore and pulled out a little baggie of dried greenery. Holding it in front of the boy's face, he asked, "Yeah? So, what's this? Oregano for your spaghetti sauce?"

The boy huffed. "Pot's legal now."

Evan chuckled. "I thought you didn't buy any?" He waved the bag again. "Yet look at this. And it's not as legal as you think."

"Yeah, well, it's not mine, so it don't matter."

The boy was grasping at straws now. Things were about to get entertaining. "I found it in *your* pants pocket."

"These aren't my pants."

This time Evan full-on laughed. "The old *these aren't my pants* defense? Really?"

"You suck." The kid rattled off a few more curses, but he stopped trying to get free.

An unmarked police car raced up to where they were—finally—and hit the brakes so fast, the back end fishtailed a little. A petite woman wearing jeans and a black sweater sprang out of the car, the badge on the chain around her neck bouncing wildly over her breasts. She ran toward them. "Get off him! That's one of my kids!"

He shook his head. "No way. He might be your son, but he is also under arrest, and Mama's badge ain't getting him outta this one. Pretty sure he broke my foot resisting. That's assault on a police officer."

Anger turned her face a bright crimson as her dark brown eyes sparked. "Not my *son*! He's one of my kids. I'm a juvenile parole officer." She stomped over to the kid's head and leaned down. "Jason! What did you do this time?"

He turned away from her. Most of the fight had gone out of him. "I ain't done nothin'!"

She glared at him. "Like I haven't heard that one before. I asked you a question, boy. What did you *do*?"

Jason scowled. "I didn't do *nothin'*."

Evan dangled the baggie between him and the woman. "Saw him buy this off Little Jimmy, then stuff it in the back pocket of his jeans."

"I told you, them ain't my pants!"

"Shut up, Jason. No one's gonna believe that." The woman stood up and offered a hand to Evan. "You can get off him now. I'll take him in."

"I'd love to stand up, but I'm not sure I can. Not My Pants here stomped on my foot pretty hard. Heard a few bones snap, and I'm pretty sure someone's gonna have to cut this boot off my foot, as much as it's swelling up in there."

Another car, a marked unit this time, pulled up, and a uniformed officer stepped out. "Marshall! You okay?"

Evan scoffed. "'Bout time you showed up. Some backup you are."

The other man scowled. "I got here as fast as I could."

The younger officer wasn't known for his speed. They'd talk about that later. "Get me up, Haynes. My foot's busted."

The woman huffed. "You just said you can't stand up."

"I can't. Not without help."

"I offered you help!" She looked like she wanted to punch him. The fire in her eyes reminded him of someone he'd known a long time ago.

"You did not!" Enjoying getting her all riled up, Evan gave her an innocent look and a shrug. "Besides, Haynes is a little bit stronger than you."

"Seriously?" She glared at him.

"You gonna take that from that pig?" Jason made a couple of oinking sounds.

"Shut up, Jason. You're in enough trouble without insinuating your PO is a barnyard animal."

He sniffed. "I weren't talkin' 'bout you."

She leaned down, holding her badge in his face. "You see this? It says stop talking before I take you to big boy jail myself."

Meanwhile, Officer Haynes had doubled over, laughing. "You busted your foot arresting that kid? What's he weigh—a hundred and ten soaking wet?"

"Can't you cut me a break, PO Baron?" Jason whined.

"Not gonna happen." PO Baron tossed her long ponytail over her shoulder. "We gonna get him up or what?" She pointed to Evan.

Haynes positioned himself behind Evan and stuck his hands under Evan's arms. "Hey, you. Can you grab his hands and help me out here?"

She gave Haynes a nasty look. "Did you just call me 'hey, you'?"

"Just help him get me off this kid." Evan stuck his hands in the air as she stepped between his feet, accidentally kicking his injured one.

Evan let out a loud groan. White-hot pain shot up his leg. Acid forced its way into his esophagus and throat. He begged God not to let him throw up. Not in front of her.

Horror filled her brown eyes as her cheeks colored with obvious embarrassment. "I'm so sorry."

"Just get me up, please." He spoke through clenched teeth. "Haynes, come on."

"On my count," Haynes said. "One, two... *three!*"

With Officer Haynes pushing and PO Baron pulling, they got him to his feet. Well, his one good foot anyway. The moment he put any pressure on his injured foot, tears filled his eyes.

No way he'd be crying in front of—well, any of them.

"I had no idea—" She nodded in his direction. "I really am sorry for being so harsh. Jason's a good kid, just a little misguided."

"Misguided. Yeah." Evan shifted so he could lean on the hood of Haynes's patrol car while the other man went to the trunk of his car to grab something.

She gave him one last look, and he could see the remorse in her eyes. On the outside she was all business, but those eyes of hers were like windows straight to her very soul. Evan found himself wanting to know more about her, but the throbbing in his foot had him so distracted he couldn't think of anything witty to say.

He forced a smile through the pain. "Don't worry about it. Occupational hazard."

She just nodded, looking like she also wanted to say something but didn't know what.

"Here, man." Haynes handed him a bottle of water and four little brown tablets. "Ibuprofen. For the pain and the swelling."

He accepted the offering and swallowed the pills with a big gulp of water.

"Come on, Jason." She turned the boy toward her car. "Call yourself a medic. I'll take him in on a parole violation and get him off your hands."

"It's my arrest," Evan ground out through the waves of nausea and dizziness starting to build.

She flashed him a brilliant, teasing smile as she looked him up and down. "Dude, you're barely standing. But if you want to spend an hour at the magistrate's office and another in booking—?"

What she said made sense, even if he didn't want to admit it. Evan finally waved her away. "Take him. Consider it a gift."

"This ain't no gift," Jason said. "My granddaddy's gonna kill me."

The woman dragged him to her car. "I don't know what you were thinking, boy."

"I know, Alayna. I'm sorry."

"PO Baron! How many times do I have to tell you?"

Evan and Haynes watched as she tucked him in the back of her car and pulled away. Alayna Baron. He liked the way that rolled through his mind way more than the nausea rolling through his stomach at the moment. The ground seemed to shift as some darkness threatened the edges of his vision.

Don't pass out. Don't pass out.

He sucked in a slow and steady breath. "I need to get a medic." Evan reached for the button on his radio.

"Gotcha covered already, buddy. I called it in while you were checking out her butt."

"I did not!" Okay, maybe he did, but he wouldn't be admitting that anytime soon.

"Whatever. Here comes a rig now." Haynes grinned, holding his hand out. "Give me your keys, and I'll get someone out here to take your car back to the station."

As he handed the other officer his keys, an ambulance pulled up. His foot throbbed, his stomach rolled, and he'd just met the first woman to even spark his interest in nearly a decade. Of course he looked like a damned fool.

"Well, isn't this just great." The darkness moved in

almost as fast as the ground he landed on with a thump.

"Hey, lady." Madeline propped herself on the edge of the old desk.

Alayna didn't even look up from her computer. Madeline liked to talk. A lot. And she didn't have that kind of time, even for her roommate. "I have a ton of paperwork to do on about sixteen different probation violations."

Madeline shook her head. "You work too hard."

Alayna looked up. "Um, it's my job."

"But it's after eight, and you aren't actually *at* work." Her friend frowned. "All you do anymore is work."

Alayna sat back in her chair, folding her arms over her chest. "Crime isn't on a nine-to-five schedule, Mads."

"You know the old saying—all work and no play makes Alayna a very dull girl."

"Sorry, I haven't heard that one before." Alayna sat forward, preparing to get back to work, but Madeline closed her laptop, knowing full well it would annoy her.

"Mads—"

Madeline crossed her arms over her chest. "You just listen for a minute. We do the same job, and I still have plenty of time for love." She blew a little kiss to a picture of her boyfriend across the room. Alayna tried not to gag.

"It just depends on who you are assigned to. You know that." She went to open her laptop again, but Madeline stood up, grabbing the computer and holding it away from her. "Don't be mad."

Whenever her friend said those three words, Alayna knew she'd end up just the opposite. Eyeing Madeline, she asked, "What exactly did you do?"

The other woman paced the small room. "You're always alone."

Alayna smiled. "How can I be alone when I have you?"

Madeline returned to perch on the edge of her desk. "You haven't gone on a single date since—"

Alayna leaned back in her chair again. "Since my fiancé basically left me standing at the altar?"

Madeline shrugged. "Well, yeah."

Alayna crossed her arms over her chest and frowned. "It's not every day a man proposes, spends months planning a wedding, and then leaves the country with his bride's maid of honor the day they are supposed to get married. That's bound to do something to a woman. Like, you know, destroy all faith in the opposite sex."

"Justin was never right for you. He only cared about himself, and you only agreed to marry him because you want a family so badly."

"I do not!"

"You do! Ever since your parents died, that's all you've ever wanted."

Alayna scowled. "Not fair, Mads."

Madeline sat down beside her, wrapping her in a hug. "Did you even love him?"

"Of course I did! I agreed to marry him. He's the one that didn't love me." She raised an eyebrow at her friend. "So forgive me for my trust issues. And this brings me back to why I shouldn't be mad?"

Madeline pulled a folded piece of paper out of her pocket and handed it to Alayna. "It's a gift. Try to take it like one. Please."

Alayna looked at the paper in her hand, then back at her friend. Madeline had a heart of gold and all the best intentions in the world, but her fix-it personality had caused more than one issue between them over the years.

She opened the paper, an email printout, and read the entire thing. Madeline watched her, blues eyes sparkling with excitement. Alayna set the paper down on her desk

"No."

Madeline's smile disappeared. "What do you mean, no?"

"I appreciate the thought, but this is not a good time for me. I have a dozen kids to manage, never-ending paperwork, and I need more than a few weeks' notice to request vacation time."

Madeline grinned again. "Already done. I cleared it with James before I even booked the reservations."

Alayna jumped to her feet. "You did *what?*"

"James is my boss too! It wasn't hard. He agrees you need a break."

"It's not your decision—or his—to make." She paced the room, aggravated that they might have seen through her tough exterior and feeling like the world's biggest loser. Her boss and her best friend, conspiring against her.

Madeline picked up the email and waved it in front of her. "Come on, Alayna. It's only four days. You love the mountains."

She had a point about that. The mountains were as close to a happy place as she had. Aside from being on a surfboard, but a winter weekend would be better spent in the mountains than in the ocean. "When is it?"

"In two weeks."

Alayna frowned. "Valentine's Day weekend."

Her friend nodded. "All the more reason to leave town. You get to avoid all the sappy memories of Valentine's Day in the past."

Score two points for her best friend. A weekend away sounded a lot better than hiding out in her apartment all weekend while Madeline and her boyfriend, Scott, did all the traditional lovey-dovey stuff.

Alayna snatched the paper from her friend's hand. "Fine. I'll go. But I'm still pissed you talked to James behind my back."

"You'll get over it." Madeline wrapped her in a joyful hug. "I'm so happy for you. You deserve this more than anyone."

Dropping back into her chair, Alayna opened her laptop. "I've got work to do now, if you don't mind."

"All work and no play...," Madeline sang as she left the room. "I've got a date with Scott. Don't wait up!"

It would only be a matter of time before Scott proposed to her best friend and left Alayna alone in her loveless life.

She read the email one more time, welcoming her on her mountain getaway. "There are worse ways to spend a long weekend, I guess."

Alayna finished her reports, gave a last check to her email, and went to bed. Madeline had gotten one thing right anyway—she was always alone. And, if she was honest with herself, alone had become very lonely.

CHAPTER TWO

ALAYNA YANKED THE STEERING WHEEL OF HER SUV to the right and prayed the four-wheel drive would do its job on the slick mountain road. The headlights behind her stayed where they were instead of passing her like she'd hoped.

She hit the gas pedal, speeding up as much as she felt safe in an attempt to put some distance between them.

As if to taunt her, heavy freezing rain began to fall, slapping against the windshield. With temperatures dropping by the minute, the icy water froze quickly upon hitting the pavement. The SUV's tires struggled to grip the smooth surface as she steadily climbed the mountain. The headlights behind closed in fast as the driver accelerated. The shoulder to her right was less than a tire width in front of the rocky face of the mountain side. The winding road made it impossible for her to safely move left. For all she knew, a tractor trailer could be coming around the bend. A head-on collision was not on tap for the long weekend.

The headlights were so close, the glare in her rearview mirror blinded her. Grasping the wheel with both hands, she prepared for impact. With a prayer on her lips that she quickly stifled, Alayna sucked in a breath. As the vehicle behind her made a sharp shift to the left and flew past her, the truck clipped the edge of her bumper. The back end of her SUV fishtailed on the ice as Alayna struggled to regain control.

The other truck disappeared into the dark as the rain switched to large, heavy snowflakes. Alayna gritted her teeth as the SUV continued to struggle to regain its hold on the road. The highway shifted to the left, and her back right tire slipped onto the shoulder and slammed against the rocky mountain face.

A loud explosion shook her core as that back tire blew out. The SUV shuddered and rocked, its balance thrown off by the destroyed tire. Hitting the edge of the pavement with bare rim made the back end kick out again. Gripping the wheel until her knuckles ached, she did her best to control the truck, but she hit a patch of ice that sent it into a complete three-hundred-and-sixty-degree turn. Facing up the mountain once more, the vehicle slid into the mountainside again, crushing the front end. The airbags deployed, smacking her hard in the face and chest. With the wind knocked out of her, Alayna's head slammed back against the headrest of her seat as the seat belt locked tight against her torso. Dizzy and breathless, she did her best to pull the remains of her vehicle off the road as much as possible. Alayna shut down the engine. Pushing the deflated air bag out of the way, she undid her seat belt and leaned back against the seat. Some start to the weekend.

Once her lungs had begun to work properly again, she opened the door and stepped out into the now heavily falling snow. Black rubber lay scattered across the white stuff on the roadway behind her, and snow blocked her view ahead.

"What am I supposed to do now?" she yelled into the chilly darkness when her cell phone showed no connection. She tripped on a piece of the rubber and fell on her backside. Too far up the mountain to safely walk back down, and too far from the lodge to not freeze to death, she sat there, next to her incapacitated vehicle, wondering if she should use the bumper as a sled and slide down the mountain.

Giant snowflakes covered her hair and jacket. Forgetting her predicament for a brief moment, Alayna stuck her tongue out and caught a snowflake, just like she used to as a kid. The entire mountain felt calm and quiet, nothing like a couple minutes earlier when some idiot had caused her current state. She had some water and some granola bars and nuts in the back of the car with a couple of blankets. Maybe she wouldn't freeze solid before the sun came up in, oh, twelve hours.

The darkness parted as headlights rounded the bend behind her car, snapping her back to her current situation. The Jeep Wrangler rolled to a stop behind her truck as the driver side window lowered. "Hey!" The driver waved to her. "You okay?"

Alayna motioned to her disabled car, still sitting on the ground. "Just fabulous. Some idiot ran me into the side of the mountain, but I found a real comfy spot to go ahead and freeze to death, so I'm good."

The man laughed as he opened the door and stepped out of his car. The medical boot he wore on his left foot caught her attention immediately. She pointed at the boot. "You're in worse shape than me. Maybe you should just stay in the car?"

He shook his head. "I'm a pro with this thing now. Are you injured at all?"

Snowflakes had already attached themselves to his dark blond hair. Alayna watched as he moved easily across the slippery pavement, only limping slightly.

"I'm fine. Aside from being stuck in the middle of nowhere in the dark during a snowstorm." With a man who could be a godsend—or a serial killer.

When he reached her, he extended a hand. Alayna debated for half a second on letting the man help her up. Still a little off kilter from her accident, she gave in though, suspecting the slick roadway would have its way with her again if she didn't.

Together they walked to her wrecked vehicle. He folded his arms over his chest as he inspected the damage to her SUV. One of the big snowflakes clung to his ridiculously long lashes. Alayna resisted the urge to wipe it away.

"It looks like your axle took a beating too. Not gonna be able to put on a spare." He laughed. "Not that it would matter."

Alayna shrugged and waved toward the front end of her truck. "Good thing I don't have one to put on.

That steam coming out from under the hood is probably gonna be a problem too. Thus, me being stranded on a mountain in a snowstorm."

He looked her over carefully, as though considering whether to leave her there or maybe wear her skin someday. His intense scrutiny made her uncomfortable even while she kind of liked the way his blue eyes darkened to match the night sky.

Something about him seemed very familiar. She just couldn't put her finger on it. Not just the fact that he kinda looked like Ted Bundy.

Shifting his weight from his injured foot, he looked from her to the damaged car.

"Do you have someone to call?"

"I have plenty of people to call. It's just gonna take them about three or four hours to get here." She pursed her lips, then frowned down at the cell phone she held in her hand. "I guess I can walk the rest of the way after I call for roadside assistance. Oh wait, I forgot, no service on my phone. Lucky me."

As though Mother Nature wanted to gloat, the wind picked up. Snow swirled around them as a gust whipped past.

"Where you headed?" the man asked, yelling over the howl of the wind.

Alayna considered for a moment whether or

not she should divulge that information, but finally decided she might be able to outrun the injured man if he did, in fact, turn out to be a killer. And she did have her gun on her if she needed it. It seemed like a better plan than freezing to death. Besides, she just couldn't shake the feeling that she'd met him before, which made her feel like he was safe enough. "Blue Ridge Lodge."

He chuckled. "Winter Singles' Weekend Getaway?"

Madeline hadn't mentioned anything about it being a singles' getaway. If this were true, her best friend would be hearing from her as soon as she had service again. What a waste of a trip—and a perfectly good vehicle. She had no intention of dating ever again, and her roommate knew that. *He* didn't need to know she'd been duped though.

Narrowing her eyes at his teasing tone, she crossed her arms over her chest. "Yeah. You got a problem with that?"

He held his hands up in mock surrender. "Not at all. My brothers signed me up for the same adventure as a gift. They think I'm depressed and it would cheer me up."

"Depressed? That's an interesting reason to send

you on a dating retreat." She shook her head, really beginning to consider the serial killer possibility.

"They're wrong." He winked.

Alayna shrugged. "My best friend thinks I need to spend more time with people my own age."

He gave her an odd look but didn't push the subject. "I can give you a ride the rest of the way. We can leave your car here for the tow truck. Then you won't freeze to death waiting. In weather like this, it could take a while for them to get up here."

Alayna looked from him to the car and back again. The temperature seemed to drop by the minute, and the snow fell faster and harder with each lost degree. She could realistically freeze to death by morning if she stayed. If she went, she could become the next missing person in the state of Virginia. Or she could be warm, dry, and fed within the hour. Her stomach growled, chiming in its vote for a meal.

She felt confident she could defend herself against the man. The storm, however, she was much less sure of that.

"Okay. Thanks. I'll take the ride. I just need to grab my stuff."

EVAN WATCHED AS SHE WALKED BACK TO HER SUV, opened the tailgate, and pulled out a rolling suitcase, laptop bag, and purse. It would be a tight squeeze in his Jeep, but he'd make it work.

He couldn't shake the feeling that they'd met before. Snowflakes clung to wavy brown hair that fell nearly to her waist. The top of her head was covered by a multicolored knit hat sporting a lavender puff ball on top. She was a full six inches shorter than he was, and Evan imagined her to be just the right height to rest her cheek on his chest if they were dancing.

Dancing? The cold had definitely begun to affect his brain.

With the weather worsening quickly, he needed to be more concerned with getting them both to the resort safely. There was no room for fantasizing about some woman he didn't know dancing with him and his stupid broken foot.

She slammed the tailgate shut and locked her truck. "Okay. I've got everything."

Evan moved carefully over the ever-icier road and popped open the back of his Jeep. "Hand me the big one first."

She handed him the wheeled suitcase. "I can keep the computer bag and purse with me up front."

Before he could reply, she'd already walked to the passenger side door and climbed into his Jeep.

Evan closed the back door and went to the driver side. Sliding in behind the wheel, he stuck the key in the ignition. Turning to his passenger, he extended a hand. "My name is Evan Marshall. And you are?"

She gasped. "As in Detective Evan Marshall of the Virginia Beach Police Department?"

He turned to look at her properly. What were the chances? It *was* her. The only woman aside from Christine to ever infiltrate his dreams and often his waking thoughts. "Parole Officer Alayna Baron."

She nodded, looking sheepish. "Yeah. How's the foot?"

"Let's just say, that boy of yours had a lot more strength than I had estimated. If I'd have known, I would have Tased him or something."

Anger quickly replaced every other emotion in her eyes. The same fire he'd seen that day on the street came to life in her, igniting a little fire of his own. "You'd have done that to a child?"

"If he deserved it." He pointed to his injured foot. "If I had, I wouldn't have been on leave for the last six weeks—and counting."

"You can't be serious? Maybe you should have

waited for backup if a scrawny fifteen-year-old was too much for you!"

He laughed, placing a hand on her arm. "Relax, would you? I'm just kidding."

It took all his willpower to ignore the small shock of electricity that jolted through him when he touched her. The feeling was so unfamiliar, he immediately thought he'd imagined it. Alayna folded her arms over her chest and leaned toward the door, putting a little distance between them. "You're kinda infuriating."

Evan laughed again. "I've been called worse."

She turned to look out the window. "Of all the people in the state of Virginia, you had to be the one to find me."

"Should I have just driven on by?" Sending up a quiet prayer for safety, he pulled out onto the snow-covered road and slowly accelerated up the incline.

"Of course not!" She rubbed her hands together in front of the heating vent. "It was getting pretty cold out there."

Her exasperation amused him, but he knew laughing would be the wrong thing to do so he turned all of his focus to the road ahead. Once he knew the wheels had a solid grip, he spoke again.

"So, your friend thinks you need to spend more time with grown-ups."

She shrugged. "At least no one thinks I'm a lonely old hermit."

"Hey!" Evan laughed. "That's not what my brothers think."

Alayna gave him a sideways glance. "What you mean is, it's not what they *said*."

Evan worked the vehicle carefully around a tight curve. The back tires spun a little but held on. The Jeep's headlights reflected on the falling snow, limiting his visibility. "Either way, we're both stuck here now for the next four days. Maybe longer if this storm doesn't stop before the roads get completely blocked."

"Won't they just plow them out?"

He shook his head. "City highways and the parkway first. This is considered a secondary road, and with no neighborhoods up here, it will be very low priority."

"Wonderful." Alayna turned and stared out the window. She didn't say much else until they saw a sign for the lodge. "One mile up ahead on the left."

"Good. At the rate this snow is falling, the road's getting tough to manage."

A large sign appeared in the headlights reading

Welcome to Blue Ridge Lodge with an arrow pointing down the wide drive among the tall, snow-covered pines. Evan slowed down and made a careful turn onto the road. A minute later, they pulled up in front of a large log structure with a full wraparound porch. White flakes of snow danced in the glow of the lanterns that broke up the darkness.

"This actually looks pretty quaint." Evan turned the vehicle off. "Better than the website. Shall we get in out of the cold?"

Alayna was already halfway out of the Jeep before he even finished the sentence. He stepped out as well and walked to the tailgate. He opened the back and pulled Alayna's suitcase out.

She took the bag and headed to the steps up to the front porch. The strong set to her shoulders and the confident way she carried herself appealed to him, despite her apparent lack of interest in him. He could see she had a strong streak of independence, maybe even to a fault. Christine had been that way and able to call him out as necessary. It had made him want her even more.

Alayna stopped at the door and turned back to look at him. "Thanks for the ride. I really appreciate it."

"You're welcome," he called after her as she pulled

open the door to the lodge and disappeared inside. With any luck, this wouldn't be their last encounter. She intrigued him, no doubt about that.

Evan pulled his own duffle and computer bag from the car and slung them both over his shoulder. Moving much slower than he wanted to, he followed the path and steps up to the wide porch. Several rocking chairs moved awkwardly in the wind. He shivered as a strong gust passed straight through his coat. "This is definitely going to be an interesting weekend."

He couldn't be sure if he was referring to the weather or the woman who'd just stirred up a long-lost flame deep in his gut.

"Welcome to the Blue Ridge Lodge!" A middle-aged woman with a wild set of salt and pepper curls greeted him as he pushed open the door and entered the large lobby area.

Alayna stood in front of the desk. To her left, a large deer head hung on a wall. Beneath it, a full-sized stuffed black bear stood with its claws raised and jaws open.

"Interesting joint." Evan stepped up beside Alayna, grinning at the woman behind the counter.

"Thank you!" the woman replied, obviously pleased with his compliment. Her curls bounced as she moved. "We love to keep things super rustic. My name is Marge. We're super happy to have you here."

Their hostess's appreciation of the word "super" totally added to the ambiance of the place. Evan motioned to the bear. "You've got me convinced. I'm Evan Marshall. I have a reservation."

"Oh, yes, Mr. Marshall. Let me just get Ms. Baron set up with a room key, and then I'll check you in as well."

"Can I use a phone?" Alayna asked. "My SUV was hit by another car, and I need to get it towed off the side of the road. Apparently, my cell phone is pretty much useless up here."

Marge covered her mouth with her hand, her eyes widening with concern. "Oh no! Are you okay? You look okay." A shadow of worry passed over her features. "But there could be internal injuries."

Alayna shook her head. "I'm fine, really. My car, though, not so much. Thanks to Mr. Marshall, I didn't have to freeze to death waiting for assistance."

Marge flashed a wide smiled and winked at Evan. "I'm so glad you finally made it to our lodge. There's a phone in your room, dear. Just dial nine to get out. There's a copy of the local Yellow Pages in the desk drawer." Marge handed her a key card. "Your room number is 202. Top of the first flight of stairs to the right."

Alayna took the key and nodded. "Thanks so much." Gathering her bags, she walked away without a word or glance to Evan.

Evan wanted to say something to her, but nothing clever came to mind so he kept his mouth shut. Alayna made him want to peel back the layers of bravado and self-protection to unearth the rare gem underneath. But he didn't want to sound like an idiot in the process. And being as out of practice as he was, he'd make an idiot of himself for sure. So he kept quiet. For the moment, anyway.

Marge nodded in the direction Alayna had gone. "She's feisty, that one." She squinted and tilted her head to the side, studying Evan. "I think you two would be good together."

Evan laughed. "Based on what? You just met both of us."

Marge leaned in and lowered her voice so only he could hear her. She tapped her temple with one long, purple-painted nail. "I've got the gift."

"The gift?"

Marge nodded, straightening and getting back to her computer. "The gift of matchmaking. My mama had it, and my grandmama and hers before her."

Evan grinned as he handed his reservation paperwork to Marge. "And your *gift* says the ice queen and I belong together?"

"Ms. Alayna is no ice queen. She's just guarding a vulnerable heart. Look at her eyes, they tell the real tale." *Like windows to her soul.* The random thought felt familiar to him, like he'd thought it before.

He shrugged. "All I know is her car was wrecked, I gave her a ride, and she barely said a word the entire time. I'm pretty sure I'm not her type."

"I think you are exactly her type. Mark my words, child, the two of you belong together." Marge handed him a room key and some paperwork. She raised an eyebrow in mock surprise. "Would you look at that? You room is right across the hall from Ms. Baron."

Evan accepted the items Marge offered. "Total coincidence, I'm sure."

Marge actually batted her eyelashes at him. "Of course it is, my dear. I tell you, some things are just meant to be."

He nodded and picked up his suitcase. "Thank you, ma'am." Evan headed toward the stairs but bypassed them and opted for the elevator. He really needed to get his foot elevated for a bit, and a flight of stairs wouldn't be optimal at the moment.

"Don't forget to come back down for dinner! Seven sharp!" Marge called after him as the elevator closed.

The doors slid open a few seconds later, and he stepped into a dimly lit hallway. Old-style lantern light fixtures added to the ambiance of the lodge. The wood chair rail and rustic wainscoting that lined the walls reminded him of his childhood home not far from there. Following the numbers on the carved wood signs, he turned right and walked to the far end. Slipping the key card into the lock, he pushed the door open and stepped into the room.

Directly across from him were large windows with the drapes pulled open. Spotlights outside the window illuminated the fat snowflakes that fell heavy and fast. The scene caused long, gray shadows to dance across the queen-sized bed. Evan flipped a switch, illuminating the brown-and-gold plaid quilt that matched the drapes. Several coordinating pillows sat against one long wall. A dresser with a flat-screen television perched on top lined the opposite wall. The door to the bathroom stood open on his left and the closet to his right. Letting the door close behind him, he moved to the bed and sat down. Leaving his suitcase on the floor, he leaned back into the pillows and stretched out on the bed.

"Well now, this isn't too bad," he said to the empty room. His injured foot throbbed. Grabbing one of the throw pillows, he shoved it under his calf to elevate it some.

A loud rumble from his stomach reminded him he hadn't eaten since breakfast. Marge had promised dinner at seven. He still had twenty-five minutes to go.

Evan folded his arms over his chest and looked around at the rustic décor of the room. "So, this is what a winter singles' getaway is like." He certainly didn't need a three-hour drive into a snowstorm to remind him how empty his life had been since Christine and Daniel had died.

The instant tension headache that appeared anytime a thought of his late wife and child crossed his mind made its appearance. Closing his eyes against the pain and memories, Evan drifted off to sleep.

CHAPTER THREE

A TEAR SLID OUT FROM UNDER HIS EYELID AS THE ringing of a phone parted the fog of his nightmare-filled nap. Evan wiped at the salty drop on his cheek as he opened his eyes and took in his surroundings. It took a moment for him to process where he was as the phone on the nightstand continued to ring.

Reaching over, he picked up the receiver and held it to his ear. "Hello?" The word came out gruff and scratchy. He cleared his throat and spoke again. "Hello?"

"Mr. Marshall! This is Marge. I wanted to let you know we're serving dinner now. I figured you'd be hungry after your long trip."

Evan rubbed the beginnings of stubble forming

on his chin. "Yes. Thank you. I guess I dozed off for a minute. I'll be right down."

"Excellent. I've set out place cards. Just look for your name on the chart and get comfortable." Marge hung up before he could say anything else.

Swinging his legs over the side of the bed, Evan sat on the edge of the mattress for a moment, thankful the pain in his foot had settled to something tolerable. After a quick trip to the bathroom, he grabbed his room key and headed back downstairs to the main dining room. The scent of home-baked cornbread wafted up the stairs, vying for control over all the other mouthwatering smells.

Opting for the elevator once more, Evan leaned against the back of the car with his arms folded over his chest. Just as the doors began to slide closed, a hand gripped the edge of one of them, forcing both doors open again.

Alayna appeared in the opening, standing there, her dark eyes deep and all her big loose curls surrounding her shoulders. Evan had never seen anyone so beautiful. She had a tough exterior but her eyes—those dark, expressive eyes—said so much, just like Marge had said. As guarded as Alayna was in every other way, it surprised him she didn't keep her eyes as shuttered as the rest of her.

"Hey." Alayna entered the elevator.

"Hey," Evan replied as the doors closed. "You fall asleep?"

She looked at him, almost smiling as she stepped a bit closer. He bet she was absolutely stunning when she actually full-on smiled. His heart skipped half a beat thinking about it. "It was a long trip. I just sat down for a second, and the next thing I know Marge is calling me and demanding I make an appearance."

Evan chuckled. "She does seem to have a way about her."

"That's definitely one way to put it." She pointed to the side of his face. "Looks like you were asleep too."

He reached up and touched his face, feeling the indentations in his skin. "Yeah. The cold air must have worn me out."

Alayna nodded in agreement. "She tell you she did a seating a chart?"

He nodded and straightened up as the elevator slowed to a stop. "Yeah," he said, wondering if the name cards had anything to do with the older woman's *gift*.

Alayna's stomach growled loudly. "I don't care if she wants me to sit in the bathroom. I'm so hungry at this point, it doesn't matter to me."

Evan followed Alayna out of the elevator and let her lead the way to the dining room. A large easel was set up with an erasable whiteboard propped on it. Marge had sketched the dining room and all its tables. Evan and Alayna searched for their names.

"She seated us together." Alayna looked over at Evan. "Why would she do that?"

Evan shrugged, knowing exactly why she'd done it. "Maybe she thinks we know each other since we came in together?"

"Oh, maybe."

"We have met before though, so maybe she's on to something?" Evan started walking toward their assigned table, Alayna following him.

Finding his designated seat, Evan sat down at the cozy table for two. Marge was definitely laying it on thick.

Alayna dropped into her seat. "Just because we had one run-in on the street doesn't mean we *know each other*."

"Is it really such a big deal?" Evan shook out his napkin and placed it in his lap. "I mean, I'm not some evil ogre or something."

She squinted at him for a moment, looking like she had no idea how to respond. "I didn't mean it like that. I'm just kinda touchy today, I guess. Between wrecking my car and the long drive—I'm just not feeling like myself."

"No worries." He smiled at her. She sort of half smiled back. Alayna Baron had his attention, there was no doubt about that.

"Do you surf?" Alayna asked.

"Not at the moment." He motioned to the boot on his foot. "But, yeah. You?"

"Every chance I get." Her eyes sparkled with her love of the water sport. It amazed him how quickly her mood changed when talking about something she clearly enjoyed. "Since I was a little girl. My dad taught me before—"

A young woman dressed all in black placed two salads on the table. "Good evening. Welcome to the Blue Ridge Lodge. I'll be back with the main course shortly. Would you prefer steak or chicken?"

"Steak," Evan and Alayna answered simultaneously. Alayna's face flushed a pretty shade of pink, accentuating her fair skin and deep, dark eyes.

The server smiled. "Good choice."

When she was gone, Alayna busied herself pushing her salad around on its plate. "I don't really like lettuce. Why do people always want to start a meal with something that looks like lawn clippings?"

Evan shoveled a forkful of the greens into his mouth and chewed them slowly. "I never considered about how much money I could save if I just raked the lawn and put the grass in the fridge."

When Alayna laughed, it totally transformed her features. He found himself wanting to make her laugh again and again just to see that relaxed, beautiful version of her.

"Here we are. Two steak dinners." The server set a plate with the meat, green beans, and a baked potato in front of each of them. "Enjoy. The way the wind has been howling, we will almost certainly lose power at some point. Cold breakfast in the morning if things keep up the way they are."

"You don't have a generator?" Alayna asked.

The young server shook her head. "Hmm, maybe we do. I don't actually know."

She walked away before either of them could ask anything else.

"Some vacation this is turning out to be." Evan stabbed a piece of meat with his fork. "Trapped on a mountain in a snowstorm was never quite on my bucket list."

"It wasn't?" Alayna's shocked expression surprised him. "It's at the top of mine."

He stared at her for a long moment, not exactly

sure if she were telling the truth or not, then Alayna winked at him and took a bite of baked potato.

Evan just shook his head and smiled. The many personalities of Alayna Baron both intrigued him and worried him. His heart still carried the scars of loss, and he had no wish to ever experience that again. On the other hand, there was just something about her, and he just had to give it a chance.

———

ALAYNA SMILED SLIGHTLY AT THE LOOK OF CONFUSION in Evan's blue eyes. They reminded her of the ocean, clear and bright when he laughed or smiled. Right now though, they resembled a storm-ravaged sea: a murky mix of gray and turquoise churning in time to his thoughts and emotions. For a brief time, he'd almost believed her bucket list comment, and that made her feel a tiny bit bad. He was so trusting, not like most cops she knew. Evan had a peaceful air about him that differed from the other men in her life—if one could consider juvenile delinquents and other parole officers the men in her life.

"So, how many brothers do you have?" Alayna asked.

Evan's brief moment of confusion darkened his

eyes another notch. Alayna wondered if there was a Pantone color to match. "What made you ask me that?"

"You said your brothers gave you this trip to get you a date."

He laughed and sat back in his chair. "I'm not sure I exactly said that. Besides, your roommate had basically the same idea."

"This makes us pathetic, doesn't it?" Alayna sipped her water. "I could use a diet soda. Water is so... *boring*."

"I think I heard there were vending machines in the game room." Evan pointed across the dining room.

"Good. I'll check it out after dinner. Thanks. So, your brothers—there are a lot of them?"

Evan narrowed his eyes slightly. Alayna shifted her gaze back to her food. "I have five. One older and four younger. Why?"

Her eyes widened, and her mouth fell open. "That's a lot of testosterone in one house. Your poor mother!"

He laughed. "She did all right. Mama ran the house like a boss. How about you?"

Alayna shrugged. "I don't have any siblings." Or any parents anymore, for that matter. After losing both her mom and dad in a car wreck when she was ten, Alayna had always been fascinated by big families.

The last memory she had of her parents played briefly through her mind. A tiny drop of salty water worked its way to the corner of her left eye. Alayna blinked it away, hoping Evan hadn't noticed.

"I always felt bad for my mom. Raising six boys on her own after my dad died. Some of us were already grown, but she still had a houseful. Gabe, my youngest brother, doesn't remember a time when Dad wasn't sick, and I know Mom felt so guilty about that." Evan ate another bite of steak and followed it with a sip of water. "I always felt a little guilty too."

"You? Why?" Alayna asked. "It's not like you were responsible for his illness?"

"No." Evan smiled at the seriousness of her tone. "Obviously not. But I did get to have him coach my baseball team and teach me to shoot."

"And Gabe didn't." The thought of a little boy she'd never met growing up without his father like she had made her sad.

"Attention, everyone! May I have your attention, please?" Marge stood in the center of the dining room, arms raised over her head as she waved her hands.

Alayna and Evan turned to face her. "What's going on?" Evan asked.

"I have no idea," Alayna replied.

"The state police have officially closed all roads in the area until further notice. No one in or out of the lodge until they lift the ban. Hopefully everything will be cleared out by the time the retreat ends, but as for now, get to know each other—we're all stuck here together." Their hostess looked especially happy about the current situation, smiling widely.

"Um, Ms. Marge?" The young server who had brought their dinner motioned to Marge.

"What's wrong, Haley, darling?"

"I, um, need you to see something." Haley's nervous expression made her look about twelve years old with her fair skin and big green eyes framed by long, shaggy bangs. Her ponytail swung from shoulder to shoulder as she looked from Marge to the lobby and back again.

Marge frowned but followed Haley to the main lobby. Alayna looked over at Evan. He seemed ready to jump out of his seat at any second.

Alayna leaned across the table. "Should we go

check on Marge? Just to be sure she doesn't need any help with anything?"

"Were you reading my mind?"

She shook her head. "Not your mind. Your body. You look like a speed skater ready for takeoff." Alayna stood up. "You coming?"

Evan stood up and pushed his chair in. "Right behind you."

Alayna led the way through the dining room, trying to appear casual, but with Evan close on her heels, she probably looked anything but. When they were in sight of the front desk, Alayna stopped and held a finger to her mouth.

"I don't know who could have done such a thing." Marge let out a little sob.

"I'm so sorry, Ms. Marge. I know how much he meant to you." Haley sniffed and wiped at her eyes with a cloth napkin that had hung on her belt. "It was Henry, wasn't it?"

Marge patted the girl on her arm. "It's not your fault. You have nothing to be sorry for. I don't know how Henry would have gotten in here, but it certainly could have been him."

"He's an awful man, Ms. Marge."

"I don't know why he thinks this will convince me to do what the court says. It just makes me want to fight him harder." Marge sighed. "All we can do now is clean up the mess. I don't need all the guests worrying about something that my crazy ex has done."

"But your daddy—"

"He was my daddy's prized possession, so let's just be glad he's not here to see this." They could hear the tremble in Marge's voice.

"What do you think they are talking about?" Evan whispered behind her.

"Let's find out." Alayna stepped out of the shadows and headed to the check-in desk. "Everything okay?" She heard Evan's boot tapping the wood floor as he followed her.

"No!" Tears poured down Haley's cheeks as she fled the room.

"Is she hurt or something?" Evan asked.

Marge didn't answer, just pointed. Alayna and Evan followed the motion, turning to see what was there.

The large stuffed black bear lay on his side on the floor. His head had been severed from his body and the stuffing pulled out of the neck. Someone had then poured a red liquid on the stuffing and floor. A large machete lay next to the decapitated beast.

"Oh, man," Evan groaned. "That bear was awesome."

Alayna elbowed Evan in the ribs. "Do you know who would do such an awful thing?"

Tears rolled down Marge's cheeks. "It has to be someone here in the lodge. The roads have been closed long enough that no one else could have gotten up here."

"You don't really think one of your employees would do this, do you?" Evan asked Marge.

Marge shook her head. "Absolutely not. It has to be one of the guests. But why would anyone want to?" Her expression switched from grief to suspicion. "The two of you took a while to get down here. Maybe you did it."

Alayna knew the woman didn't mean it, and apparently so did Evan.

He pointed to his booted foot. "You'd have heard if it were me. This thing announces me from a mile away."

Alayna raised her hands in front of her. "No red paint for me. I came down on the elevator with Mr. Medical Boot here."

The older woman waved a hand in the air. "I know. I know. I don't know what made me say that. Ignore me, please." Marge walked over and dropped to her knees, hugging the body of the bear. "I'm so sorry, Daddy. I'm so sorry."

"What happened?" Alayna looked up to see a small group of other guests gathered in the lobby. One of them moved closer to Alayna and Marge. "My name is Mary. Is there anything I can do?"

"Oh, no, no, no." Marge waved them away. "It's nothing we can't handle."

"Are you sure?" one of the men asked.

"Yes, of course." She waved at them again. "You go, enjoy your meal and getting to know each other. We're fine."

The small crowd reluctantly broke up and dissipated in different directions. Marge sighed heavily as she surveyed the damage.

Alayna stepped in behind her and laid a hand on her shoulder. "Tell me where your mop is, and I'll clean up."

Marge waved her away. "No. Haley and I will do it. You two go, mingle and enjoy your stay. My problems are not your problems."

Haley returned then with a mop and a yellow bucket with wheels filled with soapy water. "You two can go now."

CHAPTER FOUR

EVAN WATCHED THE TWO WOMEN, UNCERTAIN IF HE should insist on helping or not. He felt a light touch on his arm accompanied by a slight tingle and looked to his right. Alayna stood beside him, concern troubling her usually smooth features.

"That's really creepy." She shivered lightly. "I mean, it's bad enough someone beheaded the poor thing, but the fake blood? That's just… disturbing. Like serial killer level disturbing."

Alayna expressed his exact thoughts. Something was very wrong. Marge had made it perfectly clear she didn't want them involved. He needed time to think, to figure out what had happened and why. His detective's brain wasn't about to let that one go.

"Yeah. It does raise quite a few questions."

"It raises questions?" Alayna gave him an *are you crazy* look.

"Yeah. But they made it clear they don't want our help, so—" Evan motioned toward the dining room. "—let's go back inside. We haven't had dessert yet."

Alayna lifted a brow. "You're thinking about food right now?"

"I always have food on my mind. And I smelled some sweet cinnamon goodness coming from the kitchen. I'm guessing apple pie or maybe bread pudding."

He laughed as Alayna rolled her eyes at him. "Typical guy."

"I should be something else?" Evan glanced back at Marge and Haley. "I still feel like we should be helping them clean up."

Marge held the bear's head in her arms, cradling it to her chest while Haley squeezed water from the mop in the bucket. "I can't believe he would do something like this."

"I didn't think he'd be so awful either, Ms. Marge. Isn't there anything the police can do?"

Marge shook her head. "How can we prove it was him? Fact is, we don't know for sure ourselves."

Alayna nodded toward Marge. "That's something I never thought I'd ever see."

"Yeah. I know what you mean."

As they entered the dining room, Evan stopped walking. The lights had been dimmed, and several couples danced in the center of the floor to an old rock ballad.

"That escalated quickly," Alayna said. "What did they put in the apple pie?"

Evan shook his head. "I have no idea."

The song switched to something even sweeter and slower. Evan led the way back to their table, where they found two heaping servings of pie with a scoop of vanilla ice cream settled on top. Chocolate syrup had been drizzled lightly across the entire dessert. He found himself drawn to the dance floor and wanting to take Alayna with him.

"Goodness, would you look at that?" Alayna dropped into the chair and swiped a finger across the ice cream. Sticking the finger in her mouth, she licked the dessert away with a little moan. "This is too good."

As he watched Alayna take a second lick of the ice cream, his abdomen tightened. It had been so long since he'd responded to any woman, the sensations were almost foreign. Guilt moved in just as quickly. Christine hadn't been gone nearly long enough for him to explore those feelings, so he shoved them away. How long was long enough anyway? He had no idea. Forcing himself to look away from Alayna, he scooped a big helping of his dessert onto his fork and shoved it into his mouth. The distraction only slightly worked.

"Oh, man, you weren't kidding. This is amazing." He took another bite. "I think I've died and gone to heaven."

Alayna laughed. "You really *feel* your food, don't you?"

Marge appeared at their table. "I'm so glad you are enjoying it. The pie is my grandmother's recipe. The key is to use Blue Ridge Apples—the perfect combination of sour and sweet."

"I've never had anything like it." Evan placed a hand on her arm. "Are you okay? Is there anything I can do for you?"

Marge waved away his concern. "Haley and I cleaned up the mess. It was just an old worn-out thing my father left behind. I should have gotten rid of it years ago, anyway."

Alayna set her fork down. "Who would want to send you a message like that?"

"I'm sure it was just some sick joke. One of the employees trying to spice things up a little, maybe. Nothing to worry about. You two should be sure to dance. Enjoy the rest of the evening!" Marge twirled off into the small crowd that had gathered on the dance floor before either of them could reply.

"A sick joke?" Alayna looked as baffled as he felt. "There was nothing funny about the size of that machete."

Evan nodded. "Yeah. She could be in shock though."

"Well, I think she knows more than she's letting on." Alayna licked some chocolate sauce off her spoon while he tried hard not to watch. Everything about Alayna appealed to him on a molecular level. Each swipe of her tongue across the spoon had his body tightening. Every little moan of enjoyment had him wanting to jump out of his chair and pull her into his arms.

He took a deep breath to try to calm his racing heart and cool his rushing blood. "She's definitely hiding something, but I don't think she knows who destroyed her bear." Evan ate another bite of his dessert. Alayna seemed as interested in the event as he was. He liked that. "Maybe we can talk to Haley later, see if she knows anything."

Alayna nodded. "As long as Marge isn't nearby, I'm sure she'll talk to us."

Evan pushed his empty plate away and leaned

back in the chair. "I haven't had a meal or dessert like that in ages. Not since—a really long time, anyway." He'd almost said not since Christine had been alive. His gut twisted a little at the memory of his late wife. She had been an excellent cook. When she died, he had no interest in food for the longest time. The guilt teased him once again. Here he sat, enjoying a meal with another woman when he'd pledged his heart to Christine forever.

Until death do us part.

Death had done them part. He swallowed against the rise of emotion that thought created.

"I'm not much of a cook. But I love to eat." Alayna pushed her plate away as well. "And I can honestly say I've hit maximum capacity."

Evan laughed. "Maximum capacity?"

She rubbed her belly. "You know, like, I couldn't eat another bite even if I wanted to. There just isn't any more room."

"I know what it means; I've just never heard it used in quite that way." Evan took a sip of his water and looked around the room. "Pretty much everyone is on the dance floor now. Marge takes her matchmaking very seriously, apparently."

"Matchmaking?" Alayna raised an eyebrow.

Evan chuckled, leaning forward and lowering his

voice the way Marge had. "She's got the gift. Just like her mama and grandmama. She didn't tell you?"

"Nope." Alayna watched the couples on the dance floor. "I have always loved to dance." Her voice held a note of wistfulness that made him want to hold her right there and dance all night long.

"I'd ask you, but right now I might as well have two left feet. It's been a long day for this old man." He pointed to the boot on his foot.

"Oh, I wasn't saying—heck, who am I kidding? I totally was." Her cheeks turned a pretty coral color as she looked over at the newly formed couples swaying to the romantic song that filled the room. "I bet none of them make it until morning."

"Um, since this is a singles' weekend. I kinda think that's the point."

Alayna frowned. "That's not what I meant."

He winked at her. "Yeah, sure."

"You're absolutely infuriating." She tossed her cloth napkin at him. Evan caught it in his hand and dropped it on the table, laughing.

"I may have heard that once or twice before." Christine had said it regularly. He loved to push all her buttons, make her react to him so he could kiss away her anger. It was one of the things he'd missed most about his wife. And here he was, doing it again.

With a complete stranger who'd somehow started to awaken a part of him that he'd pretty much forgotten existed.

Alayna rose from her seat. "I think I'm going to call it a night. It's been a ridiculously long day."

Evan stood up too. "I'll walk with you. I'm done for the day also."

Together they navigated the way through all the dancing bodies. The song had switched to an upbeat, lively line dance, so getting across the room was no easy feat. At one point, he took hold of Alayna's hand without thinking and then had to ignore the little burst of heat that traveled through him at the simple contact.

As they stood in front of the elevator, Alayna let out a little sigh.

"Are you okay?" Evan asked.

She nodded, but he thought he may have seen a tear escape the corner of her eye. "Valentine's Day is a little hard for me, and seeing all the people dancing reminded me why."

That was something he could totally relate to.

The doors slid open, and as they stepped into the elevator, he said, "Yeah, me too."

The ride to the second floor was quick and quiet. The same as the walk to their respective rooms.

When they reached the place where their doors stood across the hall from each other, Evan spoke. "I enjoyed having dinner with you."

Alayna gave him a little smile, more sad than happy. "Me too. It's been awhile since I've enjoyed anyone's company. So, thank you for that."

She unlocked her room and walked inside without another word. The sound of the door closing echoed up and down the hall. Evan unlocked his own door and slipped inside, letting it close slowly and quietly.

The space seemed even more empty than it had before. Now that he'd spent the last ninety minutes with Alayna, talking and laughing, the loneliness he'd been living with felt so much more oppressive.

Grabbing his coat, a hat, and some gloves, Evan left his room again and headed to the first floor. He needed to get outside for a bit. Maybe the chilly air would clear his head and help him regain some perspective.

Music still played in the dining area as he passed through the lobby to the front door. The cold air slammed into him as he stepped outside, stealing his breath momentarily. Grasping the handrail, Evan clumsily manipulated himself down the wide stone steps to the newly shoveled sidewalk. He stood still for a moment, letting the icy wind wrap around him, whipping away all the confusion of the evening. Closing his eyes against the onslaught of cold, he pulled up an image of Christine—the one where she walked toward him down the center aisle of the church they'd both been baptized in as babies. He'd never seen anything more beautiful.

Another gust of wind blew straight through him. The memory of Christine wavered. He squeezed his eyes tight, begging her not to go, but as the image came back into focus, it was Alayna, not his late wife, that held his thoughts.

"No!" Frustrated, he opened his eyes and started trudging through the crisp snow. About ten steps in, his boot hit an icy patch. Evan's foot slipped forward, the movement taking the rest of his body up into the air and dropping him toward the icy sidewalk. He grabbed for something—anything—that would save him. Finding nothing, he hit the ground hard, knocking the air from his lungs. His left hand scraped against some ice, drawing blood.

Evan lay there, flat on his back, for the better part of a full minute. When the cold began to seep into his bones, he tested his limbs to see which ones worked still.

They all seemed functional. He stayed there for

another half a minute or so. It would be so much easier to just let Mother Nature have her way with him.

Rolling to one side, he pushed himself into a seated position and breathed deeply, hoping to fully inflate his lungs once again. Using his scarf as a bandage, he wrapped up his hand.

"Hey, man, you okay? What are you doing out here in this storm?"

Evan looked up to see someone standing over him. The stranger had on one of those huge winter parkas with the fur-trimmed hood pulled up, making it impossible to see their face.

"I slipped on the ice, thanks to my messed-up leg." Evan pointed to his medical boot.

The stranger held out a hand. "Come on, buddy, let me help you up."

Not wanting to, but worried he'd fall again and really hurt himself, Evan pushed his ego aside and accepted the offer of assistance. "Thanks."

"Get yourself inside now. This cold will kill ya." The stranger turned and began to walk away.

"Aren't you coming in too?" Evan called after him.

The man just waved as he disappeared into the darkness. For a split second, Evan nearly followed him. But then the wind kicked into high gear once more, and his body already ached from the fall.

He hobbled his way back to the lodge's entrance, gripping the rail with his uninjured hand as he climbed the steps and forced his way into the lodge against the strong force of the building storm. The ride in the elevator seemed to take forever as he daydreamed about a hot shower and plenty of ibuprofen.

When the doors slid opened and he stepped out to the hallway, Alayna stood in the doorway to her room.

"Wonderful," he muttered to himself as he limped toward his room.

"Hey, you okay?" she asked when he made it to his own door.

Evan nodded. "Yeah. Went outside and slipped on the ice. Scraped my hand and just need a hot shower."

Alayna watched him as he unlocked his door and stepped into his room. He wanted to say something, but no words would come, so he just closed the door. Leaning against the cool wood, Evan closed his eyes and took a couple deep gulps of air. His lungs burned less with each breath.

Opting to skip the shower after all, Evan dropped onto his bed fully clothed and fell asleep in seconds.

ALAYNA WATCHED AS EVAN DISAPPEARED IN HIS ROOM. His limp had been more noticeable, and his jeans were wet. When the door closed, something red stained the handle. Why would anyone voluntarily go out in the storm? Evan was an intriguing man.

The first day they'd met, Evan's amazing eyes had been all she'd remembered after their brief encounter. His name had appeared several times in the paperwork and court papers after Jason had injured him, but it had been those eyes she'd never forgotten. They reminded her of the ocean that she loved so much.

Now, after getting to know him a little more, Alayna had begun to experience something she hadn't felt in many years—the first twinge of butter-flies in her abdomen whenever he was near.

After her ex ripped out her heart and stomped on it—in Puerto Rico, with her best friend—she'd never expected to be attracted to any man ever again. There was something about Evan, though, that had her questioning her resolve to avoid love and relationships like a category four hurricane—not that she would admit that fully to anyone, including herself.

Her body's response to him annoyed her. She needed some space.

Taking the stairs to the first floor, Alayna mulled over going outside herself. The lodge made her feel caged in. A huge gust of wind rattled some windows, changing her mind. The lobby had an empty feel without the giant bear that had stood in the corner, yet the building had a peaceful quiet to it that only a heavy snowfall could cause. Alayna stepped in front of a large window and looked down across the wide front porch to the drive and parking lot. Outside security lights illuminated the sprawling property right up to the tall pine trees of the forest. She watched as the heavy snow fell, covering cars and weighing down tree branches. A mountain winter wonderland lay before her in all its serene beauty. The calm of it wrapped around her. It had been a really long time since she'd stopped working long enough to notice anything in the world.

A slight movement at the edge of the stand of trees caught her eye. She stared hard at the area. There it went again. A shadow of movement.

"Is someone out there?" she whispered.

"Could be an animal." Marge stepped up beside her. "We have a lot of those up here."

"You're probably right. I have a wild imagination," Alayna said, not believing her own statement for one second but not wanting to worry Marge. "I'm sorry if I disturbed you."

Marge shrugged. "Not at all, dear. I couldn't sleep. Just came down for some tea. Would you like to join me?"

"That actually sounds really good. My mama used to make lavender tea for me when I couldn't sleep." It had been a really long time since she'd thought of that. She'd locked away most of her memories of her parents a long time ago.

Marge led the way to the kitchen, where she picked up a shiny silver tea kettle off the stove and carried it to the sink.

"Are you and your mama close?" Marge filled the pot with water and set it back on the stove. The burner flamed to life when she turned a knob.

Alayna shrugged. "I imagine we would be if she were still alive. My parents died when I was ten."

"Oh, my dear! That's awful. I'm so sorry." Marge wrapped an arm around Alayna's shoulders and squeezed gently.

She perched on a stool at the counter. "I lived

with my grandmother until she had a stroke and ended up in a nursing home. I had a great foster family—at least the last one was. I stayed with them for three years before I aged out of the system. They never treated me as anything other than their own daughter."

Marge turned from the mugs she'd just put tea bags in and gave her an odd look. "They didn't adopt you?"

"When I turned sixteen, they offered, but I said no. I felt like I'd be dishonest to my mama and daddy if I let someone else call me their daughter. They loved me like one of their own, no doubt about that, though." The whistle blew on the teapot. Marge picked it up and filled both mugs with the boiling water.

Marge set a mug in front of her, as well as a spoon and a little sugar bowl. "You know your parents wouldn't have minded, right?"

Alayna nodded. "I know that now, but sixteen-year-old me felt so guilty about loving them, I just couldn't do it. They never let me know how much it hurt them though, and for that I will always be grateful. They just kept on like I was already theirs."

Marge nodded. "They sound like wonderful people."

"The best." Alayna sipped her tea. "This is amazing. Where did you get it?"

Marge smiled, pride gleaming in her eyes. "I made it. From plants I've grown in my gardens."

"It's the best tea I think I've ever had." She took another sip. "Yup. Without a doubt."

"I'm glad you like it. And I'm also glad you decided to attend this weekend retreat."

Alayna laughed. "I didn't have a choice. My roommate made the plans, cleared it with my boss, and sent me on my way, ignoring all of my resistance."

Marge fiddled with her mug. "You're much too young to be so… jaded, I guess."

"I'm not jaded. I just get how things work. You spend all this time trying to make someone happy, and then they run off with your maid of honor, leaving you to clean up their mess."

Marge raised an eyebrow. "Oh? Tell me more."

"Eh, nothing to tell. I was engaged. I planned on forever. He did too, just not with me."

Marge stirred her tea, deep in thought. "I think it wasn't meant be. Your perfect match is upstairs in the room across from yours." She tapped her temple. "I've got the gift, you know."

Alayna laughed, remembering Evan's comments at dinner. "What gift?"

"Matchmaking. It runs through the women in my family."

"I've never heard of that being a hereditary trait." Alayna drank the last of her tea and walked the cup and spoon over to the sink. "Thank you so much for the tea and talk. I think I'm ready to sleep now."

Marge brought her cup to the sink as well. "Oh, anytime, dear. After what happened tonight, I needed a little girl talk myself."

Alayna nodded. "Yeah, that was pretty rough. You sure you don't know who did it?"

Marge shook her head. "What would it matter if I did? We can do nothing about it until the storm passes and they clear the roads."

"Hopefully nothing else crazy happens until then."

"I concur." Marge gave her a hug. "Get some rest, dear. Breakfast is served bright and early at seven."

"Thanks again for the tea. I'll definitely be down for breakfast. Have a good night, Marge."

Marge waved as she left the kitchen. Alayna yawned three times in quick succession on her way back to her room. The day had been long, and as she collapsed on her bed, she may have had the tiniest thought that maybe she was kinda glad that Madeline had forced her to take the trip. Evan had turned out to be a decent guy, and Marge definitely didn't disappoint. Despite wrecking her car and being stranded with a bunch of strangers in a snowstorm, this weekend away may have been just what she needed.

CHAPTER FIVE

Promptly at seven the next morning, Alayna arrived in the dining room, following the delicious scent of bacon and maple syrup.

"Smells fantastic, doesn't it?"

She looked over her shoulder to see Evan standing there. Her heart skipped a tiny beat at his nearness. A slight bruise colored his right temple. Alayna reached up to touch it but stopped before making contact. "Ouch. What happened?"

"It looks worse than it is." Evan shrugged. "I must have got it when I slipped outside. Taking a walk in a snowstorm with a broken foot wasn't my smartest choice."

"Maybe some bacon and french toast will help

you get over it? Same table as last night?" Alayna pointed across the dining room.

"Sounds good to me." Evan started across the room, and Alayna followed, pleased that he wanted to sit with her again but not wanting to fully admit it to herself.

"Good morning!" Marge appeared at their table as they sat. "Did you sleep well, Alayna?"

"I did. Your tea worked wonders, thank you."

"You're so welcome, my dear." She motioned to a long table against one wall. "Breakfast is buffet style this morning. Help yourselves to anything you want."

Marge moved on to the next table. Evan gave her an odd look. "I wouldn't have taken you for a tea drinker."

Alayna shrugged. "I couldn't sleep. Neither could she." She stood up. "I'm hungry."

The tasty smells had her stomach crying out. Alayna wanted some of everything but settled on a couple of waffles, a pile of home fried potatoes, and some strips of bacon. Evan stacked his plate high with waffles, skipped the potatoes, and took about a pound of bacon.

"No worries about your cholesterol?" She pointed at the pile of meat.

He laughed. "I'm healthy as a horse."

"If you say so." She poured some maple syrup over her waffles, added a little ketchup to her potatoes, and headed back to the table.

She watched as Evan walked toward her, his limp far more pronounced than the day before. He sat down, shoving a piece of bacon in his mouth. "I may die young, but I'll die happy."

"Hey, it's your life." Alayna sipped the glass of orange juice that had appeared while they were getting food. "You really hurt yourself when you fell, didn't you?"

"I'll heal." He scooped up a huge bite of waffles and stuffed them in his mouth. "If some guy as dumb as me hadn't been out there too, I might still be lying in the snow."

"Someone else was out there with you last night? Was it another guest?" She took a bite of waffle.

Evan nodded. "Yeah. He helped me get back up. It was humiliating. I'm hoping whoever it was doesn't say anything to me today." He shoved a piece of bacon in his mouth. "Mmm, nice and crispy."

"So, it *was* another guest?"

He shrugged. "Don't know. Never saw his face. He had on one of the coats with the furry hoods, and it was dark outside."

Alayna nodded and then looked out the window by their table. "It's still snowing. We might never get out of here." She sighed, remembering her destroyed vehicle. "Not that I can get home anyway."

"I checked the weather forecast this morning. Snow isn't going to stop until sometime late tomorrow night."

"That's a pretty serious storm." Alayna took another bite of her waffles. "These are really good."

"I'm not even sure they would have towed your car yet. The roads were pretty slick yesterday. I imagine the snowstorm hasn't helped." Evan sipped his coffee. "Just what I needed this morning. Did you try it? Perfect brew."

Alayna shook her head. "I never touch the stuff."

He looked at her, appalled. "You don't drink coffee?"

"Nope."

Evan frowned. "I don't trust people that don't like coffee. It's un-American."

"Un-American?" Alayna laughed. "What's un-American is that you don't eat potatoes smothered in ketchup."

"There wasn't enough room on my plate for pota-toes *and* bacon. Life is all about choices." Evan waved a strip of bacon in the air as he spoke, then stuck the whole thing in his mouth.

Before she could reply, a loud, shrill scream echoed through the dining room. Alayna and Evan jumped to their feet and ran in the direction of the sound. Well, Alayna ran. Evan sort of stumbled behind, but she didn't stop and wait, because another scream rang out. This time it was Marge.

"What happened?" She found Marge in the lobby by one of the large windows that overlooked the parking lot. Evan joined them, as did about a dozen of the other guests.

Marge pointed out the window. Alayna looked in the direction she indicated. Through the wind-whipped snow and frost outside the window, she made out the shape of a person lying on the ground. A dark spot radiated out around her head.

"Haley." Evan appeared beside her, the young girl's name echoing her thought. He took off for the door. "Stay here!"

Alayna ran after him. "Marge! Don't come outside. We'll get her. Someone stay with Marge!"

"We got it!" Several people surrounded Marge as Evan yanked open the main door to the lodge, and a gust of really strong wind blew him backward into Alayna.

She wrapped her arms around his back, stumbling to keep them both upright as hard pellets of icy snow pummeled them. "You good?" she asked Evan before letting go.

"Yeah." He continued out into the wicked storm as Alayna grabbed the door and forced it closed behind them.

"It's gotten really nasty out here!" she yelled over the whipping winds, shivering hard. Her wool sweater barely broke the wind. "Why was she outside anyway?"

They made it to the spot where they'd seen Haley through the window. A large trash bag lay in the snow nearby, a hole torn in it and garbage strewn in the snow around it.

"Looks like she was taking out the trash." Evan dropped into the snow beside the girl and felt for a pulse. "Haley! Haley, can you hear me?"

"Feel anything?" Alayna asked, kneeling on the other side of Haley.

Evan shook his head. "No pulse. She's icy cold, and there's a lot of blood. I think she's been gone for a while."

"She's so young." Alayna touched Haley's shoulder.

"You okay?" Evan took her hand and squeezed it

lightly. Despite the freezing cold air, warmth spread through her with his touch.

"Do we bring her inside?" As a parole officer, she dealt with the living. Dead bodies didn't show up very often. Actually, not at all. Evan's touch gave her the strength she needed to stay focused though.

"We call 911 and report it." Evan let go of her hand and got to his feet. She felt the absence of his touch immediately. When his medical boot slipped on the icy white stuff, Alayna caught him for the second time, wrapping her arms around him once more. For a brief moment in time, the wind stopped whipping and the snow stopped blowing as their gazes met.

Evan spoke first, breaking the spell. "Thanks. This stupid thing is really starting to cramp my style." Alayna stepped away as Evan headed toward the main entrance, fighting through the snow.

"Are we just going to leave her out here?" Alayna asked, trying keep up and maybe wishing she were back in time, holding Evan close. She shook her head, hoping to shake the thought away.

"Until the local authorities say otherwise, yes. It's an unattended death. Could be a crime scene." Evan pushed the door open, and they went inside, fighting against the wind to get the door secured behind them once more. "I'll take some photos after I call it in. I don't want to let the weather destroy everything."

Marge stood in the lobby, sobbing, surrounded by several of the other guests. "She's dead, isn't she?"

One of the male guests stepped forward. "I'm a doctor. Does the girl need medical care?"

Evan shook his head. "I'm afraid there's nothing to be done. She's been out there a long time."

"Oh." The doctor stepped back. "I'm so sorry."

Evan turned to Alayna and, in a quiet voice, said, "Why don't you tend to Marge, and I'll make the call?"

"Okay." Alayna wrapped an arm around the crying woman and led her into the kitchen, away from the window that overlooked the body. "Come on, Marge, I'll make you some of that tea."

EVAN WALKED OVER TO THE CHECK-IN DESK AND picked up the phone. Dialing the emergency number, he waited for the call to connect.

"911, what's your emergency?"

"This is Virginia Beach Police Detective Evan Marshall. I'm staying at the Blue Ridge Lodge. One of the employees here appears to have slipped and hit her head outside. There is no pulse, her body is ice-cold, and I have no idea when it happened. We need EMS and a coroner."

"I'm going to connect you with our police department, Detective Marshall. Please hold." The line clicked and went silent. A moment later, someone else answered.

"This is Chief Roman. How can I help you?"

"Hey, Chief. Detective Evan Marshall, Virginia Beach Police. I'm a guest at the Blue Ridge Lodge, and it appears we have an accidental death on the grounds. One of the employees looks to have slipped on some ice and hit her head."

"Did you witness the accident?" Chief Roman asked.

"No, sir. Time of death unknown. But the victim is ice-cold, so it likely happened several hours ago. Probably last night."

"Here's the issue, Detective. The storm caused a bit of an avalanche on the highway up the mountain. Road is completely blocked, and I don't know how long it'll be before we can get up there. The helo won't fly in this weather."

Evan exhaled. "I have a lodge full of people here

that are freaking out. I can't leave the girl in the snow outside the window."

"There's no way we can get to you. Is there someplace on the property you can take the body—out of sight of the other guests?"

"There's several outbuildings on the property. I'm sure we can find a place. But I'm not comfortable with moving her and disturbing the scene. I just want that out there."

The chief cleared his throat. "I thought you said this was an accident, Detective?"

Evan tapped his fingers on the desk, getting frustrated. "It appears to be, but it's an unattended death, and my detective brain resists going against protocol."

"I totally understand that. Say, can you take some pictures of the scene? I assume the storm is gonna destroy whatever is there."

Evan chuckled. "Already planned on it, Chief."

"I figured, but I had to ask. I promise to call up there and let you know as soon as the road is passable." The other man sighed. "I haven't seen a storm like this move through these parts since I was a kid."

Evan sighed too. "Lucky for me, my brothers thought I was pathetic and needed to meet women."

Chief Roman laughed. "Marge told you about her matchmaking skills yet?"

Evan glanced over at Alayna and Marge. "I've heard the rumors. Okay, I'm going to get that body secured now. Don't forget to give me a call when you are able to get up here."

"Will do. Stay safe up there, y'all."

"Thanks, Chief." He hung up the phone and scanned the small crowd still gathered in the lobby. He needed to ask Marge for a couple of strong employees to help him move Haley's body.

Catching Alayna's eye, he motioned to her and Marge.

"When will the police be here?" Alayna asked as they joined him at the desk.

He held a finger to his lips and lowered his voice. "They aren't coming. Not yet, anyway."

"Why?" Marge asked, her voice trembling.

"The road is snowed over. Avalanche blocked the way. It's going to be a couple of days at least."

"So what do we do in the meantime?" Alayna asked. "We can't just leave her out there."

Marge let out a sob. "Please don't leave her out there."

"Chief Roman said to move the body to one of the outbuildings so it's out of sight of the guests." He turned to Marge and pointed to the boot on his foot. "Can I borrow a couple of your employees to help me out? This makes it real hard to walk out there. Also, I need a large tarp."

Marge wiped her eyes with a tissue and forced a smile to her lips. "I'll have Frank and Jed meet you on the porch with a tarp from the barn. Jed has keys to all the outbuildings. He'll help you find a place."

He gave her a nod. "Thanks, Marge. Alayna, can you help me get these people to disperse? They aren't going to want to watch. And I don't see any blinds on that window."

"Got it." Alayna stepped into the middle of the room. "Attention, everyone!"

The room fell silent, and everyone turned to look at her. Evan gave her a thumbs-up.

"There's been an accident. One of the employees slipped on the ice. We are going to take care of her, so there is no reason to worry. Go on ahead and follow the regular retreat schedule. Our hostess, Marge, has worked hard to make this weekend amazing."

The guests began to disperse, talking amongst themselves. Evan knew there would be more questions, but for the time being, he had no explanations for them. Grateful for the hoodie he'd put on that morning, he pulled the hood up and tightened the strings to make it stay up.

To Alayna he said, "I'm going outside to meet the guys. You got things in here?"

She stepped in close and took the strings from his hands. Tying them securely, she stared up into his eyes. He could see the worry swirling in those pools like the ocean in a hurricane. Alayna placed her hands on his shoulders and stood on tiptoe to try and look him in the eye. She barely met his chin with the top of her head. Leaning in close, she whispered, "Do what you need to do. Just be careful and come back inside in one piece. Please."

The warmth of her breath on his chin made him want to promise her everything and anything. "I will. I promise."

CHAPTER SIX

EVAN FOUND THE OTHER TWO MEN ON THE PORCH, stomping their feet and rubbing their hands together. "You guys sure you're okay with this? I know you knew Haley."

"I'm good," the older one said. "You good, Jed?"

Jed nodded. "Let's just get her out of the snow. Haley hated the cold. I can't bear to think of her out here alone."

Frank held out a folded tarp. "I grabbed this from the barn. I hope it's large enough."

"I'm sure it's fine. Let's get this done." Evan led the way to the body, wind-whipped snow slicing against his skin like tiny razors. Hard snow crunched under their feet. Evan's injured foot slipped a few times, but he managed to stay upright. The last thing he needed was to slip and fall again.

"Jesus, Mary, and Joseph." Frank made the sign of the cross as he stood over Haley's remains. "Her poor mama is gonna be heartbroke."

"There's people watching." Jed pointed at the window, where a few of the guests were still congregated. "Give me one side of the tarp."

Frank did his best to unfold the tarp with the wind whipping it around. A dust devil of snow swirled between them and the building, making it nearly impossible for Jed to grasp the blue material. Evan grabbed one corner and tugged.

"Keep it low. It might help." They pulled the tarp out and moved Haley onto it. After they wrapped the body, Frank led the way to one of the outbuildings built into the side of a hill.

Evan muscled the door open. The wind caught it, and it slammed against the side of the building. "Come on!"

Frank and Jed passed through the door and set the tarp-wrapped body on the floor.

Jed exhaled, his breath forming an icy cloud. "It's really cold in here."

"A hundred years ago, this would have been used as a root cellar. See the vents up there?" Evan pointed to a row of shutters along the top of the front wall. "They let heat out, and the ones along the floor let cold in."

"He's totally correct." Frank pointed to a set of shelves across the room. "Years ago, those were filled with jars of Ms. Marge's mimi's canned food. Jams, soups, veggies—you name it, she had it." He walked over to the unit. "I used to sneak in here as a kid and take a jar of peaches every so often. Mimi pretended not to know, but I'm sure she did."

He stopped talking for a moment, reaching up to one of the top shelves. Pulling down a single sheet of paper, he looked at it and frowned.

"Whatcha got there?" Jed asked.

"I'm not exactly sure." He handed it to Jed. "Does this look like a map of the lodge property to you?"

Evan stepped in beside Jed as the other man studied the roughly drawn document for a moment. "It sort of looks like it. Is there anything else up there?"

Frank reached up and felt along the length of the shelf. When he found something else, he brought it down for them all to see.

"Hey!" Jed snatched the ring of keys from Frank. "That's the extra ring of master keys that went missing last week! How did it get up there?"

"Are you absolutely sure that's what they are?" Evan asked. "Any way they could have been up there a while?"

Jed shook his head. "Absolutely not! See the labels? Ms. Marge had all the locks changed a couple of months ago, and I labeled the keys. That's my handwritin'."

"And somehow they ended up out here in this empty building." Evan frowned. "Why did she change the locks?" Something didn't sit right with him; he just couldn't quite put his finger on it yet.

"Her ex-husband. He's been threatening Ms. Marge since she appealed to the court about him getting half her lodge. Had her real scared. He had keys to everything, so she had them all changed."

"Why would he get half?"

Jed shrugged. "Don't know. Guess that's how divorce works in Virginia."

Evan clasped his hands together and blew into the palms to warm them. "We should get back in the lodge. Temperatures are dropping fast."

"Where's your jacket, man?" Jed asked, motioning toward Evan's hoodie. "You're gonna freeze to death."

"I'll be fine as long as we get back inside." He folded the makeshift map and tucked it in his pocket as he walked out the door and waited for the other two men to follow. It took all three of them to pull the door closed and latch it against the howling wind gusts that had definitely increased in speed.

Evan's injured foot already felt ice-cold. Snow had worked itself into all the openings of his boot, and his heavy wool sock had soaked through. If he didn't warm it up soon, he'd have to add frostbite to his list of injuries.

It took so long to make it back to the lodge that Evan shook violently as they entered the warm lobby. His teeth slammed together so hard, his jaw hurt. Alayna ran toward him, carrying a heavy wool blanket. "You were gone forever. I nearly went after you."

"We f-f-found some-something." The violent shivering felt like it got worse as she wrapped the blanket around him.

Frank and Jed headed to the kitchen with Marge and several other employees. The last few remaining guests dispersed to other activities, leaving Evan and Alayna basically alone in the lobby.

"Here." She led him to the fireplace and helped him to sit on the large stone hearth. Evan stretched his injured leg out along the hearth, letting the heat from the fire reach it. His toes were numb. His fingers too. The warmth felt amazing, even as he kept shuddering. Sitting on the floor in front of him, Alayna took his right hand in hers and rubbed it quickly, trying to warm the icy skin. After a few minutes, she took his left hand and repeated the process. He wanted to be able to say the tingles he felt came entirely from the return of blood flow, but that might have been a bit of a lie.

Worry darkened her eyes as she studied him. "Why would you go out there without a jacket and gloves?"

"You did the same thing earlier."

Alayna shook her head. "For like two minutes. And I'm wearing a heavy sweater over thermal underwear. I'd bet money you've got a tee shirt on under that sweatshirt."

He grinned at her, his teeth still clattering a little. "You're worried about me."

She frowned at him. "I am not. I just think you were being reckless. We have no way to get you any help if your foot gets seriously frostbit."

He nodded slowly, still grinning. "So, you *are* worried."

She dropped his hands on his legs. "I'm *not* worried. Just rational. Are you warming up at all?"

"Yeah. I think I'll move to the sofa right there." He

slowly swung his leg off the hearth and shifted his body from the stones to the nearby couch.

Alayna grabbed another wool blanket from the top of a wood chest and put it over him.

"Thank you." He patted the sofa beside him. "Sit with me for a few minutes? You know, body heat and all to help me warm up?"

Alayna gave him a look that questioned his sanity but sat down anyway, tucking the second blanket in around him as she settled beside him. "You aren't shaking nearly as much. How does your foot feel?"

"I'm no longer worried about it freezing off."

She studied the fire. "You must truly be in God's grace."

Evan glanced over at her. "What's that supposed to mean?"

"You are already hurt. Last night you slip and fall on the ice, and today you go running around in a blizzard with a hoodie and a medical boot to protect you from the weather."

He chuckled. "Child's play. You should have seen me when I was a kid. Regular trips to the ER—my parents basically ran a tab there."

"Are you just clumsy or a real risk-taker?"

"Let's just say, most of my trips began with '*Hey,*

Mom, watch this.'" He pointed at his injured foot. "This one, however, was not my fault."

She punched him lightly in the arm. "I still feel really bad about that. If it helps, the kid ended up back in front of the judge, who revoked his probation and put him in juvie."

Evan laughed. "It doesn't make me feel better to know a kid that young is already so confused."

"Even though I've been doing this job for years, it still upsets me to see kids like Jason throw their lives away for drugs."

ALAYNA PACED IN FRONT OF THE FIREPLACE, THE familiar emotions associated with her job returning from the short hiatus they'd been on since she left her home.

"I'm sorry he ended up back in detention." Evan grabbed her hand and tugged lightly toward the couch.

Alayna let him pull her back to her seat. "I tried everything with him. He just didn't care. So many of them get caught up in the endless cycle."

"You obviously care about your clients. I don't

blame you for this. My foot got broken before you even showed up."

She sighed. "I got into that field to help people. I wanted to be a cop for as long as I could remember. Juvenile services seemed like a place where I could help kids get back on the right track instead of just arresting them and handing them off."

"I wouldn't say we just arrest them and hand them off." He sounded a little offended.

"That's not what I meant. Your job is very important. I just wanted something where I formed relationships with my clients, you know?"

He nodded. "I get it. I'm sure you're great at your job."

She leaned her head back against the couch. "I just can't believe we both ended up here."

"The Lord moves in mysterious ways. That's what my mother would have said." Evan reached up and toyed with a lock of her hair. The action was a simple one. It surprised her that she liked it, since she'd been so anti human interaction for so long.

"Have you warmed up yet?"

He nodded, still playing with her hair. "I can feel my toes again, so that's good."

"I'm glad." She wrapped her hand around his where his fingers tangled in her hair. "Your hand feels normal now too, and you aren't shaking anymore."

He remembered the map. Pulling it from his pocket, he handed it to Alayna. "We found this in the root cellar."

She opened it up and stared at the marks on the paper. "What is it?"

"I think it's a map of the lodge grounds. We found it with a set of master keys that had gone missing a few days ago."

Confused, she studied the paper. "Why?"

He shook his head. "I don't know. But Jed, one of the guys that helped me, said the keys went missing last week. After Marge had all the locks changed to the lodge."

Alayna looked up. "She had all the locks changed?"

Evan nodded. "According to Jed, she did."

"Okay, so Marge changed the locks, and someone stole the keys, hiding them with this sketch in an empty shed."

"That's the gist of it."

She shook her head. "This is all too weird. First the bear, then Haley. Now this."

"And the man I saw last night."

"The one that helped you when you fell?" Alayna

asked.

He nodded. "Instead of heading into the lodge, he actually headed toward the barn."

Alayna pursed her lips and raised an eyebrow. "That's odd. I mean, even if you are used to the snow and cold, this storm is no joke. Downright danger-ous, actually. Especially in the dark."

"Yeah." Evan tugged one of her curls lightly. "It could be something—or mean absolutely nothing. Do you realize your curls bounce right back after I tug on them?"

Alayna laughed and nodded. "Um, yeah. They've been with me my entire life."

"Excuse me for interrupting." Marge joined them, holding a steaming mug. "I thought this hot choco-late might help thaw you out."

Evan reached up and accepted the mug, licking at the pile of whipped cream she'd put on top of the warm liquid. "Thank you, ma'am."

She lay a hand on his shoulder. "Thank you for taking care of our girl. I'm still so sad, but it helps to know that she doesn't have to lie out there in the snow and cold indefinitely."

Evan put his hand on hers. "I never would have allowed that."

"I heard you on the phone with the chief of

police. You're a police detective in Virginia Beach?" If she weren't mistaken, Marge looked a little worried.

"I am. And Alayna here also works for the city as a juvenile services officer." He laid his other hand on her arm briefly, causing her heart to skip half a beat with the contact.

"Well, I feel much safer knowing the two of you are here. After what happened to my bear and then to Haley—"

She broke off with a sob that felt less than genuine to Alayna.

Shaking off the suspicion, Alayna rose and gave the woman a hug. "I'm so sorry for your loss, Marge. I can't begin to understand how you are you feeling, but if there is anything I can do, please let me know."

"Yeah, me too." Evan pushed the two blankets off of him. "I think I'm about warm enough now."

"Well." Marge's eyes sparkled with mischief. "You could help me get a round of karaoke going in the event room. Everyone is still a little upset about Haley. It might help to lighten the mood some. After all, this is supposed to be a fun getaway. Being snowed in was unexpected, but we can still have a good time."

Alayna looked at Evan and raised an eyebrow. "I'm game if you are."

He pursed his lips. "I don't know. I might do more harm than good. Singing isn't exactly my best talent."

"Please?" Marge said, folding her hands as if in prayer.

He glanced from Alayna to Marge and back again. "How can I say no to two beautiful women depending on me to save the day?"

Alayna swatted him lightly with a throw pillow. "Save the day? I wouldn't exactly go that far."

"I'll make an announcement and let the guests know we will get started in, say, thirty minutes?"

Evan stood up. "That will give me time to go get some different clothes on. These jeans are still kind of damp."

Alayna nodded. "Okay, Marge, see you in thirty minutes."

She waited for Marge to be gone before asking Evan, "Are you sure you're up to this? You were looking pretty blue when you got back in here."

He gave her the sweetest smile. "I had a good nurse." Evan leaned down and pressed a light kiss to her forehead. "Thank you for warming me up, Alayna."

The simple contact created an anything but simple reaction within her. A long-forgotten emotion radiated through her with the warmth the kiss brought on. Evan winked as he straightened up and walked away.

CHAPTER SEVEN

ALAYNA STAYED BY THE FIREPLACE AS EVAN LEFT THE room. The roller coaster of emotion she'd been on for the last hour or so had worn her out. Adrenaline from finding Haley and worry for Evan mixed with the feelings she got when he smiled at her or touched her. Forget about her knees going weak when he'd kissed her forehead just now. She felt like a sixteen-year-old with her first crush.

After her wedding that had never happened, Alayna had sworn off relationships. Being abandoned on her wedding day, in her foster family's church, where the priest had looked at her in pity, had been enough humiliation to last a lifetime. She had no interest in putting her heart out there ever again.

That had been her plan, anyway. Until this stupid singles' weekend had happened. Trapped with a handsome police detective with no way to get home and weird things happening put her in an interesting position of wanting things she'd convinced herself she could live without. Evan Marshall had some darkness of his own, though. She'd seen it in his eyes when they'd found Haley, and again when he'd looked at her as she warmed his hands by the fire. Until that little kiss to her forehead, his smiles had been somewhat guarded, his friendly demeanor still keeping her at arm's length.

Marge's voice carried through the speakers of the lodge, inviting everyone to the event room for some karaoke and cookies with cocoa. Even in the wake of tragedy, Marge seemed to know what to do to keep the mood up.

Alayna walked to the event room, stopping for a moment in front of the same window where they'd first seen Haley. It seemed dark outside with the heavy gray snow clouds parked over them. She watched the snow fall as the wind swirled it into tiny tornadoes, until a different kind of movement caught her eye. Off to the edge of the large circular drive, she thought she saw a person. Pushing up close to the cold glass, she peered out into the storm, looking for the black jacket she could have sworn she'd seen a moment ago. A full minute passed before she gave up and admitted she could have been mistaken. Continuing on to the event room, Alayna put the image out of her head.

Marge stood at the front of the room, prepping the karaoke equipment. As Alayna debated where to go next, she heard the telltale clomp of Evan's medical boot against the wood floors. She turned to greet him just as he stepped up next to her. Dressed in a pair of navy blue running pants and a long-sleeved gray T-shirt that hugged his firm chest perfectly, he looked like he'd stepped out of the pages of an ad for a department store—a look she definitely approved of.

"Feeling better?" she asked.

Motioning to his outfit, he replied, "Dry clothes make all the difference."

Alayna smiled. He made her want to smile a lot, she noted. "I bet they do."

"You ready for this?" He directed her toward Marge's setup, placing his hand lightly at her lower back.

She concentrated on not reacting to his touch, even as it heated her skin. "As ready as I'll ever be. What are you planning to sing?"

He pointed to a large screen. "I don't think we have a choice. I hope you know your Sonny and Cher."

The lyrics to the duet "I Got You, Babe" filled the screen. "Interesting choice, Marge."

Marge laughed. "I trust you two to have fun with this one."

"Oh, we will!" Evan took her hand and pulled her to the little stage.

"I'm not so sure about this anymore." Alayna held back when they got to the raised area. "I didn't know she meant a duet."

"You're not afraid, are you?" Evan teased. "You just have to channel your inner '70s love child, and you'll be fine."

Alayna laughed, pursing her lips and tucking her hair behind her ears. "Right. I've totally got this."

"Come on, you two!" Marge waved them up. "Let's have a round of applause for our first couple!"

The other guests cheered and clapped. "You can do it!" someone called out.

Marge handed her one microphone and the other to Evan as the first few notes began to filter out of the machine. Panic started to take over the moment she accepted the microphone. Evan winked and gave her that amazing smile of his. "You got this."

She faced the screen scrolling the words to the song and took a deep breath. It took a couple of lines for her to find her groove, but by the time they got to the chorus, she'd almost forgotten they had an audience. As they worked their way through the next verse, Evan took her hand and twirled her around the small platform. They gushed through the second chorus, and by the end of the song, Evan had her in a deep dip. The crowd cheered and sang along, and for a few minutes she forgot about dead bodies and angry snowstorms. Evan set her on her feet, grabbing her hand and pulling her into a bow. Tiny ringlets of hair clung to the moisture that had formed on her forehead and at her temples, but that didn't stop Evan from planting a huge kiss on her lips. The kind that smacked loudly and elicited another round of cheers from the crowd. She could feel the flush from the singing deepen into another kind of blush as her lips tingled from the kiss.

"We did it!" he said as he pulled away. "You were amazing."

She nodded, still feeling a tad unsteady. She raised a hand and touched her mouth with her fingertips. "*We* were amazing."

They handed the mics back to Marge and stepped off the low platform as another couple took their place. She knew Evan had only kissed her as part of the performance but that didn't stop her from wanting him to do it again.

Evan wiped his forehead with his sleeve. "Whew! That's the best workout I've had in months. I need a big glass of water."

"How is your foot doing?" Alayna asked as they exited the room and headed toward the table in the lobby where the staff kept lemon water in a dispenser. The feel of his lips on hers lingered. She tried to resist reaching up and touching her lips. Or grabbing him around the neck and kissing him again.

"It's not my foot I'm worried about. It's my everything else. I'm not lying when I say I've become a bit of a couch potato since it happened."

They stopped at the table, and each poured a cup of water, drank it, and then refilled. Alayna glanced over at his trim, muscular form. "I can't imagine you being a couch potato."

He waved a hand down the length of his form. "This is leftovers."

She narrowed her eyes at him. "What do you mean, leftovers?"

"I used to work out a lot. After my wife died, I

had a lot of anger. Worked it out with the weights in my garage."

He'd been married. And then widowed. Maybe Evan was older than she'd thought.

"I'm so sorry you lost your wife. Were you married long?"

"Just a little over a year." His usually clear blue eyes darkened with emotion. "Not nearly long enough."

Her heart ached for the pain he obviously still felt over losing his wife.

"It's a long time since she died, but it still feels so fresh, you know?" He drank another cup of water, then tossed the cup in the trash. "I think I'm going to go to my room and elevate my foot for a while. See you at dinner?"

She nodded. "I don't usually miss meals."

He smiled, a tiny bit of the sadness still lingering in his eyes. "Same table?"

"I'm sure Marge wouldn't have it any other way. Do you want me to bring you a sandwich or something from lunch?"

He tugged lightly on a strand of her hair, wrapping the length of it around his fingers. He seemed to like doing that—and truth be told, she kind of liked it too. The action sent a little tingle through her body, particularly when his fingertips brushed lightly against her cheek. "I'm not real hungry. I think I just need a nap. It's been a long morning."

"Okay. Dinner it is, then. You know, I have a book I've been wanting to read. I think I'll go upstairs for a bit too." She headed to the elevator, Evan beside her as she walked.

"If it weren't for what happened to that girl, this would be a beautiful weekend." Evan pointed to the snow still falling outside the windows. "I've always loved the snow."

The elevator opened, and they stepped inside. "Not me. I'm a beach girl. I hate to be cold, and this storm brings a whole new meaning to cold."

"There is no cold like mountain cold, I suppose," Evan replied. "I grew up not far from here, you know. Ever been to Staunton?"

"No. But I hear it's nice."

"It is. I loved growing up in the mountains, but I do love the feel of the beach. It has its own healing powers. Toes in the sand and all that. Nothing like the Atlantic Ocean to remind you of your place in this world."

"How very true." She liked the way Evan saw things. At their rooms, they parted ways. "See you at dinner." Alayna gave him a little wave.

He responded with that same sad smile he'd had when they talked about his wife. "Knock on my door when you're heading down. I'll go with you. Beat Marge to her dinner phone calls."

"Will do."

Once alone in her room, Alayna collapsed on her bed and stared up at the ceiling. Evan had been married. The despair in his eyes when he talked about his wife told Alayna he'd loved her deeply. Evan had some serious baggage, much more than someone as young as he was should.

Of course, so did she. She might even be more damaged than he was, in some ways. Being abandoned on her wedding day—well, she'd never seen it coming, and it had left her feeling broken. Talk about carrying baggage around—like living with the fact that she hadn't even been enough for the man who had *asked* her to spend his life with him. And the humiliation. Oh, the humiliation.

She hadn't been to her family's church since that day. She and God didn't exactly see eye to eye anymore. And she'd basically written off every friend she'd had prior to the wedding. The embarrassment had just been too great. Her heart couldn't take the constant reminders of all the things she and Justin had done together with their friends. Forget about ever falling in love. She and love didn't see eye to eye anymore either.

So, why did Evan Marshall make her think about all the things she thought she'd never, ever think about again?

AS SOON AS HE HIT HIS ROOM, EVAN GRABBED A bottle of ibuprofen and took a couple of the tablets. Between nearly freezing solid and then dancing around with Alayna, his entire body ached, not just his injured foot.

It had been a while since he'd felt his age—not that thirty-one could be considered ancient by most standards. At the moment, it sure felt that way though.

Sitting down on the small sofa, he grabbed the remote and turned the television on. After clicking past all the morning shows and reruns, he turned it back off. His mind couldn't focus anyway. It kept returning to the woman in the room across the hall.

After his wife died, Evan truly believed that he'd had his one and only chance at love. For ten years, he held on to the memories—and the heartbreak. He wore them like a protective armor around his heart.

Don't get close to anyone, and they can't break your heart. In barely twenty-four hours, that armor had begun to show some chinks in the form of a petite parole officer with a sharp wit and beautiful, expressive eyes.

It bothered him that she affected him so much. It felt dishonest to his wife's memory. Never mind that of his child. He deserved to be alone forever for not being able to keep her and their son safe.

How long would he punish himself for something completely out of his control?

That was what his brothers had asked as they handed him the reservation information for this trip.

Looking up to the ceiling and wishing the answers were written there for him, he closed his eyes. "Do I deserve a second chance at love?"

A booming thunderclap or some other notable response sure would have been nice. He had no idea what he should be doing. Grieving for his wife and child? Or enjoying the new feelings Alayna brought back to life for him? If only there were rules for that kind of stuff.

Rotating so that he could stretch out on the length of the sofa, he hugged a pillow to his chest as his eyes closed and he slid into the oblivion of sleep.

The next thing he knew, someone rapped loudly on his door. The clock on the cable box read six forty-seven. Dinner started at seven.

"Hold on!" Hobbling across the room, he looked through the little peephole to see the woman who had been in his dreams standing outside the door.

She knocked again. "Wake up, Evan. You're going to miss dinner!"

Grasping the knob, he yanked the door open. "How did you know I was napping?"

"I didn't. Until now." She pointed to his face. "You have lines on your cheek again."

He could feel the heat filling his face. "Oops. I just need to wash up and comb my hair. Do you want to come in a minute and then we can go downstairs together?"

Alayna looked at her watch and then back at him. "Okay. But don't take too long. I wanted to check in on Marge before dinner."

He stepped aside as she entered, then closed and bolted the door. He left her and walked into the bathroom. "Marge is pretty tough."

"Maybe so. But it's obvious she loved Haley. And her death is going to hit her hard, once all this is over and she is alone."

He pulled a brush through his messy hair. "More

than likely. It is pretty sad. Haley had so much of her life left to live."

"I just can't figure out why she'd go out in a nasty storm to dump one bag of trash."

Splashing some cold water on his face, he patted it dry with a hand towel. "I'm sure she's done the same thing hundreds of times before. Probably never even thought about it. People who grow up in the mountains look at weather like this as an inconvenience."

Alayna laughed. "It's a heck of a lot more than inconvenient. I'd take a hurricane over this garbage any day of the week."

"Really?" he asked. "Hundred mile an hour winds are pretty nasty too."

"Yeah," she replied. "But at least there is nothing to shovel. No ice to worry about."

He couldn't help but laugh. "So, you prefer flooded roads, power outages, and trees falling over?"

"Like I said, no snow. No ice. And it's not cold." She laughed. "I know, I'm weird."

"I've never met anyone else that sees things quite the way you do." Evan pulled his T-shirt off and stepped from the bathroom to grab a polo out of the closet, running straight into Alayna. Her palms landed flat on his chest, sending all sorts of sensations all over the place. When she looked up at him with those green eyes, he lost all rational thought. Reaching up, he touched her lip lightly with his fingertip. "I want to do something now I haven't wanted in a very, very long time."

She blinked once then ran her tongue lightly over the spot where his finger had just been. "Oh?"

So many feelings descended on him like a tornado of emotion. His brain could barely process it all as he wrapped his arms around her and pressed his lips to hers.

Everything else disappeared; the heartbreaking memories of his wife, the lodge, even his busted foot. All he could think about and feel was Alayna in his arms. Time stood still until Alayna broke the kiss.

"Wow," she whispered. "You kissed me."

"Yeah." Evan took a deep, steadying breath, trying to calm the upheaval in his abdomen. "I—yeah." He exhaled, at a total loss for words. His thoughts were a jumble of maybe he shouldn't have done that and maybe he should do it again.

Alayna stepped back into the open space of the room, her face flushed and her eyes glassy. "I-I'm sorry. I was—I mean, I couldn't hear you, so I moved closer. I didn't expect you to…." She touched a finger to her lips. "And then…."

He grinned as he stepped toward and pulled her into his arms again. He toyed with some of the waves hanging loose down her back. "You sure you weren't snooping?"

"Oh no! I'd never do that. I promise. Besides, I had no idea you'd walk out here half naked." She pushed lightly against his chest with her palms.

Evan let her go again, reluctantly. "I just wanted a clean shirt." Stepping back into the bathroom, he pulled a light blue polo over his head, checked his hair once more, and then shut the light off. "I'm ready now if you are."

Alayna had returned to her usually cool, even façade. "Yep. I'm famished. I should have eaten more today." She rubbed her abdomen. "My stomach has been complaining for about an hour now."

Unlocking the door, he held it open and made a sweeping motion with his arm. "After you, m'lady."

She did a little curtsey while looking up at him through her eyelashes. "Thank you, kind sir."

CHAPTER EIGHT

HIS BODY STILL FELT FAIRLY STIFF AS HE AND ALAYNA walked to the elevator. Though he hated to admit it, the exposure to the freezing cold had definitely had its way with him. The nap eased some of it, but what he really needed was a solid night of sleep.

"You ready to go home yet?" he asked as they stepped into the elevator. As soon as he said it, he knew it was a stupid thing to say.

She shrugged. "I'm okay here for now. Not like I have any way to get there."

"I'm pretty sure I can find room for you in my Jeep once this storm clears."

Alayna smiled. "Thanks. I appreciate that. The fact still remains though, my car is wrecked and I'm going to have to deal with that sooner rather than later. I checked in with the towing company. They were able to get my truck off the mountain before the storm blocked the way, but they had to use a flatbed because the back end was so mangled."

The elevator stopped at the first floor, and they stepped out into the lobby. His senses were immediately assaulted by deliciousness. Marge stood at the reception desk, talking to one of the guests. She waved to Evan and Alayna.

"It looks like she is doing better," Alayna said, waving back.

Evan returned Marge's wave as well. "Yeah. It's probably shock, though. We need to keep an eye on her."

"I know. Dinner smells heavenly." Alayna inhaled deeply. "Fresh bread. Maybe some stew? Or a pot roast."

"You're passionate about food, aren't you?" He clasped her elbow lightly, simply from the desire to touch her, and steered her into the dining room.

"I am. My foster mom is a fantastic cook. I miss it. I can hold my own, but there's just something about food when someone else cooks it, you know?" They sat at their usual table. "I feel like pretty much all we've done since we got here is eat. Not that I'm complaining."

He nodded and gave her a little wink. "It definitely hasn't been the trip I thought it would be. But I'm okay with how things are going so far—you know, aside from nearly freezing to death and Haley."

"I was pretty mad at my roommate for making me do this. And, of course, there's the issue with my car. But I like Marge." She looked up at him and smiled. "And you're not so bad either. Nothing like your reputation back home."

Now that interested him. He leaned forward on his elbows. "My reputation back home?"

Alayna spread her napkin on her lap. "While you were napping, I called a friend of mine in the department. She had some interesting things to say."

"Let me guess—Evan Marshall is a playboy. The forever bachelor that loves and leaves after only one date." He'd heard it all at one time or another.

Alayna frowned. "How'd you know?"

"I work with a bunch of guys that like to sling insults for fun. Those are some of their favorites. The irony of it is, I rarely date. And I haven't been with anyone since my wife."

He'd gotten used to the rumors and really didn't care what others thought of him. Usually. For some reason though, he *really* cared that Alayna knew the rumors weren't substantiated in fact.

She reached across the table and laid her hand lightly over his. "I'm glad to hear this. I was really struggling to reconcile the Evan Marshall she described with the man I've met. I hoped you weren't trying to fool me or something."

He turned his hand over so their palms touched. She traced the lines on his wrist with her fingertip, sending his nerve endings into tiny little explosions. "Never. What you see is truly what you get. I'm rough around the edges, but not at all like people seem to think."

Two bowls with steaming hot contents settled on the table in front of them. They both moved their hands away as a basket of freshly baked rolls appeared as well. "I hope you're hungry. Tonight's stew night."

Their server wore a name tag that read Christine. She was several years older than Haley and lacked the younger woman's easy smile. And she had his wife's name.

"Thank you so much." Evan smiled and winked,

laying a hand on her arm briefly. Just like that, Christine's entire face transformed.

"You're definitely welcome. There's more if you want it." And then she was gone from their table.

Alayna grabbed a roll and smeared some butter in it. "I can see where your reputation came from."

"Because I'm nice to people?" Her comment bothered him way more than it should.

"Relax, Detective. I just saw how well you can work a moment. Our server was cranky and short when she got here but practically gushing when she left."

He took a big bite of stew and chewed it slowly, trying to decide how to end this conversation and get the spotlight off him. "People like to feel good about themselves. Basic human interactions are just one type of validation. Plus, my wife's name was Christine."

THE SILENCE THAT SETTLED BETWEEN THEM WITH Evan's announcement made her incredibly uncomfortable. Searching for something to say, she ate a spoonful of her stew instead to buy herself a little more time.

"This has got to be the best stew I have ever had. I need to see if Marge will share the recipe with me." Alayna took another bite of the meat and vegetables. "Mmm... so good."

Evan stabbed a chunk of potato with his fork. "It sure is better than the canned stuff I buy at the supermarket."

"You buy canned stew?" She raised an eyebrow. "That's just—well, I have no words really."

Evan laughed. "Widower, remember? It's not worth all the effort to just cook for myself."

Alayna waved her fork at him. "Now that's where you're wrong. You could cook one big meal on, say, Sunday, and eat for days. Without the sodium and preservatives."

"Preservatives keep me fit and healthy." He winked. "Works for canned stew, so it should work for me, right?"

She dropped her fork on the table and looked at him. "You're joking, right? You don't actually think—?"

Evan's face transformed into a teasing grin. "I'm kidding. Had you going there for a moment though, didn't I?"

"Maybe." She took a long sip of the ice water in her glass. "Sometimes it's hard to tell with you."

As they finished dinner, Alayna actually didn't want the night to end, something that surprised her. Ever since her non-wedding, Alayna had found peace and security in being alone. Being alone meant being safe. Her heart couldn't get hurt because she didn't give anyone the chance to touch it.

Evan had begun to chip away at the brick wall she'd erected around her feelings. She enjoyed his company. They had a lot in common, and his easy way balanced her more high-strung personality.

Evan leaned back and rubbed his abdomen. "I feel like all I've done since I got here is eat."

"We already covered that." She leaned back and rubbed her own stomach. "Besides, it's not true. You nearly froze to death. That's something."

"If things keep on the way they have been, I'll leave this lodge fat and frostbit."

"Oh, please." Alayna waved away Evan's comment. "You look great." As soon as the words left her mouth, she felt the heat in her face.

Evan winked at her. "In that case, I think I'll go ahead and have dessert then."

The lights blinked. Once. Twice. The third time, the room was flooded in darkness. A chorus of cries filled the room.

Marge's voice rose above the others. "It's okay,

everyone! We have a generator. One of my men is going out to get it started as I speak."

The dining room fell into an eerie silence as they all waited for the lights to return. The howl of the wind outside added to the nervous atmosphere. A minute or so later, the lights flashed and then turned on.

"Yay!"

"Hallelujah!"

"We have lights!" The man at the next table pulled his dinner partner to her feet and began to dance her around the space. Other couples joined in, and before long, the happy, relaxed mood had returned.

"I'd love to ask you to dance, Alayna, but I think my foot has had enough excitement for one day."

That blush returned to her cheeks as she studied the fork in her hand. One of the tines had been bent slightly. She tried to straighten it with her fingers, with no success. "Oh, I'm not much of a dancer anyway."

"I don't know. I think you held your own during our karaoke performance."

Actually, she used to love to dance—before the wedding reception that never happened. Their server set two slices of cheesecake with fresh fruit on their table. Alayna scooped up a bite on her fork and ate it.

As soon as the creamy dessert hit her mouth, she moaned. "Wow. This is *so* good."

Evan took a huge forkful and stuck it in his mouth. "Oh my gosh," he mumbled around a mouthful of creamy goodness and fruit.

His eyes rolled up toward the ceiling, making her laugh. "Should I leave you alone with your cheesecake?"

"Remember, I've lived alone for a long time. And baking is so not in my skill set. My wife handled that."

He tried hard to hide it, but Alayna caught the shadow that passed over his expression at the mention of his wife.

"I wonder how she'd feel knowing you are surviving on microwave dinners and canned stew." She ate the last bit of her cheesecake and pushed the plate away. "That was amazing."

"I know. I want to pick the plate up and lick it."

Alayna held a finger to her lips. "Shh. We can't do that here. Everyone will know our dirty little secrets."

Evan grinned. "It's like you've known me your whole life."

Alayna shook her head, smiling. "Nope. I just know a good meal. Some nights I cook three-course dinners, and others, I eat cereal. Dry. I don't even bother with the milk."

"Oooh, a lady of adventure." Evan turned serious. "Did you lose someone too?"

She frowned. "Oh, I know exactly where he is. On a beach in Puerto Rico with my former best friend."

"He left you for your best friend?" Disbelief darkened his eyes. "How could he do that?"

Alayna traced little circles on the tablecloth with her finger for a bit before deciding to go ahead and lay it all out. Taking a deep breath to steady herself, then letting it out slowly, she looked at Evan as she spoke. "He practically left me standing at the altar on our wedding day and hopped a plane with the maid of honor—my former best friend. She never showed up to the church. We thought something terrible had happened. My foster father and some of the other guests were going to look for her. What we found instead, on the windshield of my car, was a note that said he didn't love me and couldn't live a lie anymore."

As she shared her most devastating moment in her life, Evan's expression changed from interest to anger. Not the pity she'd expected. The looks of pity had always been the worst part of the whole horrible event. Evan didn't look at her like she was pathetic. He looked like he wanted to hunt her ex down and arrest him.

"He did that?" Evan reached for her hand and wrapped her fingers with his. "How could anyone ever hurt you like that?"

She shrugged. "Apparently, I'm disposable."

He squeezed her hand lightly. "Not even the slightest bit."

Alayna stood up, pulling her hand from Evan's. The dining room suddenly seemed too loud and congested. "I need a little space. I think I saw a checkerboard in the game room. You up to having your butt kicked?"

Evan stood up and pushed his chair in. "You should know, I was the Blue Ridge checker champion when I was in middle school."

"The Blue Ridge checker champion?" She narrowed her eyes at him. "You can't be serious."

He held his palms up. "Hey, I'm just trying to do due diligence by letting you know what you're up against. I have the blue ribbon at my mom's house to prove it."

"Come on, blue ribbon boy." Alayna left the

dining room, instantly feeling better as soon as she entered the empty lobby. "I'm about to challenge your title."

CHAPTER NINE

THE CHECKERS SAT ON A BAR-HEIGHT TABLE WITH stools that matched. All the game pieces appeared to be hand carved from hardwood.

"I didn't notice this earlier." Evan picked up one of the checkers. "These are beautiful."

Alayna climbed onto one of the stools and motioned to the other. "Stop procrastinating. It's time to put up or shut up."

"As you wish, Officer Alayna." Evan sat on the other stool. "Be prepared to lose." He slid one of the red checkers into a new box on the board.

Alayna responded by moving one of the black checkers. "Will you cry if you lose?"

Evan shrugged as he slid another checker out of

its starting point. "I have been known to shed an occasional tear. This is a serious sport, you know."

Alayna raised an eyebrow. "Are you this competitive over everything?"

Evan slid another checker into place. "Only things I'm passionate about."

Something in his tone said he wasn't talking only about checkers anymore. Alayna studied the board, selecting her next move carefully and avoiding Evan's stare.

"Nice play," Evan said as her checker jumped over his and she scooped it up. "But not as nice as this one." He jumped two of hers and swept them to the side.

"Ouch. I definitely didn't see that coming." She pursed her lips and studied the board, finally making her move.

"You set me up." Evan frowned. "No matter where I move, you're going to get my checker."

She smiled her sweetest smile and pressed her hand lightly over her heart. "Little ole me? Set you up?"

Evan moved one of his pieces. She was so excited to capture another of his that she moved too fast. Her fingers brushed his, sending a tingle through her. She froze as he wrapped his hand around hers, both enjoying the moment and wanting to pull her hand away just to protect her heart.

She looked up to see him staring at her. "Evan?"

"I'm still trying to wrap my head around the fact that any man blessed enough to have you love him would see fit to abandon you the way your ex-fiancé did."

"It was a long time ago. I'm over it. Really." Even to her own ears, she sounded like she wanted to convince herself more than him.

When had she become so pathetic?

Evan smiled, lifting her fingers to his lips and kissing them. "I don't think you're pathetic."

Alayna pulled her hand away. "Um, did I say that out loud?" The feel of his kiss still tingling on her skin.

"It's okay. I won't tell anyone."

She smiled. "It's been a really long time since I enjoyed the company of anyone of the opposite sex. Truth be told, though, you do make me nervous sometimes."

Evan reached up and pressed his palm to her cheek. "I never want you to feel uncomfortable with me."

"Not uncomfortable. Nervous. Like teenage girl with a crush nervous." She felt the heat in her face and looked away, totally embarrassed. That seemed to be happening to her almost hourly since meeting Evan.

Evan slid off his stool and stood beside her. "Alayna. Look at me."

She turned slightly so they could make eye contact. "It's okay, Evan. You don't have to say anything."

"My wife died ten years ago. No one has ever made me feel like a clumsy teenager like I did with her. Until now."

Alayna turned so she faced him completely. "Oh?"

He leaned in close. "Yes."

He was going to kiss her again. Alayna really wanted him to kiss her. She closed her eyes and held her breath.

"Excuse me?"

Alayna sighed. They both looked over to find Marge standing a few feet away. She looked frantic as she wrung her hands in front of her.

Alayna left her stool and walked over to the other woman. "What's wrong, Marge?"

She pointed toward the door. "In the kitchen."

"What's in the kitchen, Marge?" Evan asked, heading that way.

"Frank." She sniffed. "On the floor. There's blood."

Alayna and Evan took off toward the kitchen. Alayna got there first, stopping at the door. Evan and Marge joined her.

"Marge? Did you touch anything?"

The older woman shook her head. "No. I went in to set a tray of dishes by the sink and found him. I think he's dead." Tears ran down her face. "He can't be dead! Not after what happened to Haley."

Alayna gave Evan a nod, and he went into the kitchen while she stayed with Marge. She took her by the shoulders and looked her in the eyes. "Stay here, Marge. Please."

Marge nodded and moved over to lean on a wall, dabbing her eyes with the hem of her cardigan.

Alayna pushed through the swinging doors. "Evan?"

"Over here."

She followed the sound of his voice to a spot on the far side of the kitchen. Frank lay on the floor, a small pool of blood by his head.

"Careful, Alayna. The floor is wet over there."

She looked down at the floor, and sure enough, she stood in the middle of a puddle of water. "Where did this come from?"

"I don't know. But it's probably the reason Frank slipped and fell."

"Is he...?" She stepped in a bit closer, careful not to touch the counters or step on anything that could be important.

Evan nodded. "Yeah. No pulse, and his skin is already starting to show signs of mottling. Looks like when he slipped, he could've hit his head on that prep counter there."

Alayna spotted some proof of Evan's theory on the corner. "There's definitely some red stuff up here. Looks like blood."

"This means two potentially accidental deaths in one day," Evan said, standing up. "Something's not right here." He pulled his cell phone from his pocket and started to snap photos. "I think Chief Roman will want these."

"I feel that way too. But what else could it really be?" Alayna glanced around the room, then lowered her voice. "Do you think there's a killer among us?"

"I honestly don't know what to think. I mean, Haley slipping and falling and freezing to death, that really could have been an accident. But this? I suppose it could have been an accident as well. But the fact that it happened after Haley—after we found the map and the keys—that's what concerns me."

Alayna agreed. "You should call it in, like you did this morning."

"I will. I want to get the body out of here first though, so none of the other guests see him."

"I'll get Marge. Hold on." She went back to the kitchen door and motioned for Marge to join her.

"He's dead, isn't he?" Marge dabbed her eyes with her cardigan again. "First Haley. Now Frank. What's happening here?"

"I wish I knew." Alayna squeezed her hand lightly. "Two accidents in one day just seems too coincidental."

"I know." Marge sniffed and dabbed her eyes once more. "Does that mean there is a killer staying at my lodge?"

"Honestly, I don't know what we're up against. I do know we need Jed to help move the body out of the kitchen before the other guests see him. Do you think he can handle that?"

She nodded. "I already told him to go help. I can too, if you need me."

"We may. Frank is going to be a little heavier than Haley."

Alayna led the way back to the kitchen. When they arrived, Jed already had a tarp spread over the body.

"I hope you don't mind, I went out the back door and grabbed this from the barn." Jed motioned to the outside door at the back of the kitchen then the tarp.

She stepped in next to Evan and motioned toward his injured foot. "Marge is here to help me and Jed. I think you should consider staying inside this time."

Evan frowned. "I'm fine."

Laying a hand on his arm, Alayna spoke quietly. "I know you are. And I know you are perfectly capable of doing this. But it's icy outside, and now it's dark. We just don't need to risk anyone else getting hurt until we figure out what's going on here. I need you to be okay."

He looked for a long moment at the place where her hand touched him, then nodded. "Fine. Okay. Jed knows what building it is."

They wrapped Frank in the tarp and carried the body out the back door of the kitchen. The trek to the outbuilding exhausted her. With the wind whipping around them and icy bits of snow pelting her face, it was close to impossible to keep her footing on the slick ground. When they finally made it, Jed unlocked the door and they pretty much fell inside the building, Alayna tripping on the other tarp-wrapped body on the floor. Frank's heavy form fell to the floor with a thump.

"Oh!" Marge stumbled and fell, landing face-first on Haley's body. She scrambled to her feet, backing into the wall of the shed. "I'm so sorry!"

"It's okay, Marge. Come on, let's get you back to the lodge." Alayna led Marge toward the door.

"Go ahead." Jed waved them out the door. "I'll lock up and be right behind you."

Marge nodded, and together they braved the nasty weather once more. Evan met them at the back door. "Everything okay?"

"Yeah," Alayna said. "Jed's right behind us."

Evan closed the door but watched out the window. "I see him. You get her warm, and I'll wait for Jed."

"Okay. Find me when you're done?"

He nodded. "I will."

SITTING OUT WHILE ALAYNA AND MARGE HELPED JED lug the body to the shed stung his ego, but he knew Alayna had been right. His foot still ached from the trek that morning. If he hurt himself again, with no way to get to a doctor, the damage might be irreparable.

As Jed reached the lodge, Evan pulled the door open to let the other man inside.

"I swear it's even nastier out there than it was this morning." He stomped the snow off his boots and pulled off the coat he wore, hanging it on a hook by the door. "Good thing you didn't risk that broken foot of yours."

Evan grunted. "Yeah. I guess. You okay, man?"

Jed shrugged. "I've known Frank my entire life. After my old man died, he stepped up and became the father figure I needed. I don't know what all happened in here, but I know Frank knew this kitchen like the back of his own hand. The water on the floor doesn't make sense to me. Not one bit."

"Something doesn't sit right with me either, but I'd like to keep that from Marge for the time being."

"I hear ya. I won't say a word." Jed grabbed a mop and began to swab the floor.

Evan left Jed and went in search of Alayna. When he finally caught up with her, she was sitting on the sofa in front of the fireplace, holding her hands up in front of the flames.

She looked over at him when he sat down next to her. "Marge went to her room. My fingers always take so long to warm up."

"Here. Let me help." He pushed her palms

together and wrapped his hands around hers. "Wow! You're freezing!"

Alayna laughed. "It's just my fingers. I don't know why it happens."

He rubbed his hands over hers to elicit a little friction. Holding her hands felt so natural, like he was always meant to do it. "Cold hands. Warm heart."

She gave him a questioning look. "What exactly does that mean?"

Evan shrugged as he continued to warm her hands. "My mom says it. An old wives' tale or something, maybe?"

"I'm not quite sure that's what it is." Alayna sighed. "Or how true it is."

"If you're trying to say you're coldhearted, I'm not buying it." He stilled his hands but didn't release hers.

"That's not what my ex says." Her eyes shone with unshed tears. She pulled her hands from his.

"Your ex is a fool."

Alayna stared at the fire. She tried to pull her hands from his, but held on, keeping the connection between them. "You don't know anything about me, Evan."

"Maybe not. I'd guess we have a lot more in

common than you think, though." He reached over with one hand and touched her chin, gently guiding her to look at him again. "I know you've had your heart broken, same as me."

"Not the same at all. Your wife died. My fiancé left me for my best friend. On our wedding day."

Evan toyed with a stray curl of her hair, as had become his habit whenever he could get away with it. "I know. I'm so sorry. I will never understand that."

"He left me a letter. Said he needed someone with passion. A woman that showed emotion and had a sense of adventure. Apparently, I'm boring, cold, and passionless. He couldn't see the rest of his life with me in it. So he and the maid of honor hopped the plane to our honeymoon together and haven't been back since."

He slid over on the sofa so he could wrap his arm around her shoulders, hoping she wouldn't try to move away. "He sounds like a coward and an idiot to me. Not man enough to take responsibility for his own actions, so he put the responsibility on you."

Alayna laid her head on his shoulder. "It's been three years since it happened. You'd think I'd have gotten over it by now."

He gave her a little squeeze, breathing in the

scent of her shampoo. "There's no time limit on grief."

She laughed without humor. "As much as I sometimes wish he was, he's not dead."

"No, but the love you had for him, the life you thought you would have, are dead. That's just as traumatic, if not more."

"I suppose." She picked at a thread on her jeans. "I don't know why it's getting to me so much today."

"Stress will do that."

Alayna looked up at him. "Stress? This is the most relaxed I've been in years."

Evan chuckled. "I actually believe that. But your car is wrecked and you are stranded on a mountain in the middle of a snowstorm with bodies showing up around every corner."

"Just another day in paradise." Alayna sighed. "I know you're right. The whole thing is just crazy. I feel like something more is happening here than freak accidents."

"Me too. I think there's foul play involved, and it has all my cop radars firing at once."

She nodded. "Yeah, mine are going crazy also. It's hard to imagine a murderer among us, but at this point, anything is possible."

Alayna sat up and stretched her arms over her

head. He missed her closeness acutely enough that it made his heart skip half a beat. "We need to keep an eye on things. Patrol the lodge at night and make sure all the guests stay safe. I'm worried what could happen when the sun goes down. It's even easier to hide evil in the dark."

"I agree. Let's do it together."

Her smile warmed him from the inside out. "There's safety in numbers, you know. Especially when the company is good."

"I couldn't agree more."

CHAPTER TEN

E‌VAN MOTIONED TO THE WINDOWS. "T‌HE STORM clouds make it so much darker at night."

"The storm should be coming to an end by morning. At least I hope so." Alayna held up her phone. "I checked the forecast earlier today. When the Wi-Fi was still working."

A couple of the other guests wandered into the lobby and over to the elevator. A small group of five or six followed close behind.

"I guess this evening's festivities have come to a close." He pointed to the group.

"Looks that way." Alayna stood up from the sofa. "I'm going to go check on Marge and let her know that we're going to keep watch tonight. Just in case."

Evan stood up too. "I'll make a round of the

doors and windows while you do that, make sure everything is secure. And check in with the police chief."

"Okay." Alayna left him alone in the lobby. It didn't take long for the remaining guests to disperse to their rooms. Only the distant ticking of the huge cuckoo clock that hung over the check-in desk broke the silence.

Evan checked the main doors first, sliding the large dead bolt into the locked position. Wind rattled the heavy wood, making an eerie noise as it blew through the tiny spaces around the frame. From there he secured the large french doors off the dining room and events room then headed to the kitchen to check the service entrance. Along the way he made sure each window was locked. The idea briefly crossed his mind that he might actually be locking a killer *in* with them, but he dismissed it as quickly as it presented itself.

While in the kitchen, Evan made himself a cup of coffee and carried it to the lobby where he waited for Alayna to return. He'd worked his way through most of it by the time she showed up.

He raised his mug. "I'd have made you one, but I didn't think you drank coffee."

She smiled. "I'm actually more interested in that

tea I had with Marge last night. Mind if I make a cup before we settle in to guard duty?"

Evan finished off his coffee in one swallow. "Not at all. I'll pour another cup for the road also."

A strong gust of wind rattled the windows as they returned to the kitchen, catching his attention. Alayna pulled out a mug and went to the pantry for the container of tea. "I really prefer a hurricane to a snowstorm."

Evan laughed. "I'm not so sure about all of that. I live in a flood zone by the beach."

"That's your mistake." Alayna filled her mug with water and set it in the microwave. She rubbed her arms. "At least hurricanes are warm. I feel like I've been cold since my accident."

Evan poured the last cup of coffee from the pot, shut the machine off, and set the pot in the sink. "I can definitely agree with you on that. I'm just starting to feel my toes again."

"I wonder if Marge has any cookies around here." Alayna went back into the pantry and emerged with a container of chocolate chip cookies. "Want one?"

"Of course." Evan grabbed three and shoved one in his mouth. "Mmmm." He moaned.

She laughed. "Maybe I should leave you alone with those."

"I told you, I've lived alone for a very long time. Store-bought cookies just aren't the same." He popped another one in his mouth and moaned.

"I haven't had home-baked cookies in years either." Alayna took two from the container, then set it on the counter. "Maybe we'll make a stop in later."

"I checked all the doors while you were with Marge. Everything down here is secure."

"How about a check of the floors?" Alayna took a sip of her tea. "Then we can hang out by the fire in the lobby and keep an eye on things."

Evan carried his coffee and his one remaining cookie toward the elevator with Alayna following close behind. The lodge only had three floors of rooms. They took the elevator to the top floor and walked the length of the hallway.

"Everything looks good up here." They stopped in front of the elevator, and Evan pushed the down button. Once they were inside, he leaned against the wall and sipped his coffee. "Do you think we have a murderer among us?"

Alayna shook her head slowly. "I just don't know. Both deaths could have been accidents. The weather is horrible. If Haley slipped and hit her head, knocking herself out, it wouldn't take long to freeze to death. She only had on her uniform and a light jacket."

The doors opened, and they stepped out on to the next floor. Evan motioned to her to lead the way. "Frank's death could have been accidental too. There was the water on the floor. He was a big dude. The head injury could have been enough. At least, I think so." He sighed. "Scratch that. What I mean is, I *hope* so. And, that feels so wrong to say, on so many different levels."

At the end of the hall, they paused their walk, and Evan pressed his nose to the glass of a large window. "Look at the snow swirling in the spotlights. It's so pretty, I almost forget how dangerous it is."

Alayna stepped in next to him and peered through the glass. The snow danced in little spouts as the wind seemed to blow from every direction. He became acutely aware of her proximity, wanting to wrap an arm around her and pull her in close. Instead he took a step, putting a tiny bit of space between them.

"What's that?" Alayna pointed out into the storm.

"What?" Evan followed the direction she pointed. "I don't see anything."

"Something moved. I saw it. Over there." She tapped the glass with her fingernail.

"Where? I don't see anything." He pressed his face in closer and watched along the tree line. "Wait! I *do* see something."

"Do you think someone could be out there?" Alayna pressed her cheek to the window beside him, closing the tiny gap he'd just created. He breathed deeply of the citrus scent emanating from her hair. He should have guessed Alayna wouldn't be a floral girl. The fresh citrus suited her so much better.

"In that weather? I sure hope not. But after that guy helped me up when I fell the other night, it's possible." He stepped back, needing to break the spell of her presence and regain his focus. "Let's finish our walk through and get back to the ground floor, just in case."

It didn't take long for them to return to the lobby. Alayna headed to the kitchen for another cup of tea, so Evan grabbed a couple more cookies.

"I really think someone was out there." Alayna pulled her cup from the microwave and sampled the heated liquid, both of her hands wrapped around the mug. "Mmm… so good. And warm."

"How could anyone survive out there in this weather? They were walking off into the woods, on foot—you know, if we actually saw a person." Evan took a bite of one of his cookies and chewed slowly and swallowed before speaking again. "It could have been an animal. Maybe a deer."

"Maybe." Alayna settled on the couch in front of the fireplace. "This couch is amazing. It's my favorite place in the lodge. Actually, everything here is pretty amazing."

"My bed is perfect. This really is a great lodge. I'd like to come back in warmer weather. I bet the hiking is phenomenal." He walked over to the hearth and grabbed a couple of logs to lay on the dwindling fire. They had a long night ahead of them, and the fire made things a little cozier with the storm still raging outside.

"I bet it's beautiful here in the summer. I might like to come back too, one day."

Evan leaned back into the cushions and stared into the fire.

"I wanted to take our honeymoon in the mountains, but Christine was adamant we travel to an exotic, faraway place." He couldn't believe he'd just said that. Being with Alayna was so easy, he actually felt comfortable discussing his wife. He hadn't been this relaxed with a woman since, well—since Christine.

Alayna turned her mug in her hands. "Oh? Where did you end up going?"

"St. Lucia. Paradise, she called it."

"I've never been anywhere. My honeymoon would have been my first international trip. Now I have no *desire* to go anywhere."

Evan picked up her hand in his and held it. "His stupidity likely saved you from a huge heartbreak later."

Alayna chuckled. "Worse than nearly being left at the altar in a floor-length wedding gown and a cathedral-length veil?"

"Believe it or not, yes. I would bet my next paycheck he's cheated before and would do it again, many times in your future."

She frowned. He hated that he'd made her sad, but he knew he spoke the truth. Once a cheater, always a cheater had been his experience. "You're probably right. When I look back over our relationship, all those times he forgot to call or showed up hours late—it's not like accountants have that much fun at work."

Evan squeezed her hand lightly. "An accountant? I can't imagine you with someone like that."

"Apparently, neither could he." She took a sip of her tea and stared into the flames.

"You'll meet the right guy and forget all about him."

She looked over at him. "How about you? You've been alone longer than I have. Do you want to fall in love again one day?"

He leaned his head back against the sofa and looked up at the hewn beams that formed the ceiling. "I used to say absolutely not. Christine was my one and only love, and when they died, I figured that was it for me."

Alayna shifted so she could look at him, questions in her eyes. "They?"

"Our baby." He swallowed hard against the rise of emotion. "Christine died in childbirth. I lost my entire family in one awful moment. I buried them together so they'd always have each other." He felt the tears run down his face as he looked away from Alayna. She shouldn't have to see him fall apart like that. The past was the past, and there was nothing he could ever do to change it.

So why did his heart feel like it had broken all over again, just thinking about that day?

"I'm sorry. I didn't mean to dump all that on you." Evan wiped his eyes with the sleeve of his shirt.

"You have nothing to apologize for. And you didn't dump anything on me. You listened to my sob story. At least you have a real reason to be sad." Moving across the couch, Alayna wrapped her arms around him and laid her head on his shoulder. "I'm so sorry, Evan. I can't even imagine what that was like."

If he spoke, the tears would return, so instead Evan rested his cheek against her head and watched the flames dance in the fireplace, enjoying the kind of closeness he'd really missed.

ALAYNA FELT THE SLIGHT TREMORS THAT PASSED through Evan as he tried to hide his emotions. She never in a million years would have guessed the heartbreaking story behind all the playboy rumors she'd heard.

Sure, she'd been humiliated, standing there all alone reading a hastily scribbled note while every person she knew waited for a wedding that would never happen. Her heart had been broken but not destroyed. Evan's very soul had been crushed. His heart torn from his chest and buried alongside his wife and child.

They sat there like that for a long time, watching the flames crackle and dwindle. Finally, Evan sat up and shifted slightly. "I should put more wood on the fire."

"I suppose so." She didn't want him to move. The warmth they created sitting together rivaled the heat of the fire, and she liked it.

Evan stood and grabbed a log, situating it inside the huge stone fireplace. He placed a second one over it. They both watched as the flames caught.

"That should hold us for another hour." He sat back down beside her, close enough that their thighs touched and she could lean on his shoulder again if she wanted to.

Alayna pulled a blanket over them from the arm of the couch. "Even with the fire, it's like I can feel the windchill all the way to my bones."

"Maybe this will help." As she'd hoped he would, Evan wrapped an arm around her shoulders and pulled her close to his side. He pressed a light kiss to the top of her hair. "I'm feeling less and less annoyed with my brothers for sending me here."

"Me too. I'm not so annoyed with Maddy for tricking me into this trip." She felt like a sixteen-year-old girl on her first date with all the butterflies taking flight in her abdomen.

"How have we worked for the same city all this time and never crossed paths?" Evan had his fingers looped in the waves of her hair, sending little shivers down her spine.

"Oh, but we have, Detective Marshall. Remember?" She laughed and pointed to his injured foot.

He shrugged. "That was not my finest hour. I prefer to forget it ever happened. Virginia Beach isn't all that large; we should have run into each other somewhere else along the line."

She raised an eyebrow. "You mean us? The two most antisocial people in the city?"

Evan yanked one of her curls lightly. "When you put it like that, it does sound pretty ridiculous."

Alayna nudged him with her elbow and laughed. "Yeah."

"I'm glad we have finally crossed those paths." Evan moved closer as his blue eyes churned like a storm-ravaged ocean.

"Me too," she practically whispered as she closed a little more of the distance between them.

The tension between them took on a life of its own as Alayna found herself wanting him to kiss her more than she wanted to take her next breath. Her heart rate sped up exponentially with every millimeter that disappeared between them. When she could feel the warmth emanating from his flushed face against her own, she took in a breath and waited.

The lights went out, swamping them in darkness.

"What happened?" Alayna glanced around the lobby, but the only light still there came from the fire.

"The storm, I guess." Evan stood up and moved to look out one of the large windows that overlooked the driveway.

Alayna followed him. "But the power is already out. A generator shouldn't do this."

As soon as she spoke, the lights came back.

Evan turned away from the window. "It could have been a hiccup in the system." His voice held a touch of doubt that gave Alayna an uneasy feeling.

A loud slam from the kitchen made her jump. "What was *that*?" She reached for the gun on her hip under her sweatshirt. "Something's not right here, Evan."

He held a finger to his lips. "I know," he whispered as he pulled a gun out of a holster on his ankle. "Stay here, and I'll go check the kitchen."

She shook her head. "No way. I'm coming with you. Backup."

Evan didn't argue, so she followed him, gun at the ready as they moved through the dark lodge.

A strong gust of cold air hit them as they entered the kitchen. Another slam, much louder this time, sounded.

"The back door is open," Alayna barely whispered behind Evan. He nodded slightly in response.

"I'm going to close it."

They halted in front of the large double sinks. Over the commercial wash basins sat a wide picture window that overlooked the parking lot. Alayna waited as Evan moved slowly toward the open door. Out of the corner of her eye, she caught a flash of movement. A shadow seemed to be making its way toward the main doors. She slipped back out of the kitchen and returned to the lobby. Footsteps sounded on the wide front porch. Alayna stood at the edge of one of the windows, watching as a shadow moved slowly across the snow.

The door handles rattled. Alayna spun, gun pointed at the doors. "Who's there?"

Footsteps pounding down the front steps were the only reply. Alayna unlocked one of the doors, yanked it open, and ran out into the storm.

CHAPTER ELEVEN

"I KNOW I SAW SOMEONE." SHE CAUGHT SIGHT OF TWO sets of footprints on the steps—one going up and one going down—but there was no human in sight.

Alayna slowly worked her way down the slippery steps, one hand on the rail and the other on her gun. When she reached the ground, she pulled a small flashlight out of her pocket that she'd tossed in there as she walked out of her room earlier. She had no choice but to use the light. With the power out and the moon buried behind storm clouds, the darkness felt all-consuming. The prints continued to the right, away from the kitchen end of the building and toward a large barn. As the wind blew, the marks became less and less clear. She followed them all the way to the old barn. The doors, one hanging off its top hinge, flapped in the wind. Shining her light in between them, Alayna found fresh boot prints in the layer of blown-in snow.

"I knew I'd seen someone." Shining the light around the mostly empty room, she stepped in just enough to get out of the wind. Along one wall she found various picnic tables, grills, and other outdoor items. Extra tables and chairs for the dining room were stacked in one corner. The other wall had a few empty stalls and a couple of closed doors. Obviously the building had become a storage area for the main lodge. She could see no reason why anyone would be in there in the middle of the night, though.

Alayna walked over to the closest door. A tarnished copper sign hanging on a nail in the wood read OFFICE. With her flashlight hand, she tried the doorknob. It turned easily. Pushing the door open, she searched the space beyond with her flashlight, expecting to see standard office fare. A desk sat against one of the walls, a wood chair tucked under it. What she didn't expect to see was the electric lantern perched on top of it, next to a half-drunk soda and an open bag of chips. The cot on the opposite wall holding a pillow and wool blanket caught her by surprise also.

"What is all this?" Alayna entered the room and

walked toward the cot. She barely made it two steps when something hard hit her on the back of the head. Her knees buckling, she crumpled to the floor, lost in a sea of blackness.

"ALAYNA? COME ON, BABY, WAKE UP."

Her body moved slightly, like she rocked in a chair. Everything felt so cold. Her toes, her fingers, everything. And her head really hurt.

"Please, Alayna. Open your eyes."

Evan. Why did he sound so far away? With one hand, she reached toward the voice.

Evan clasped her icy-cold hand in his. "There she is. Just open your eyes now, please. You're freezing." She could hear the relief in his voice.

"Mmm...," she groaned. Her head ached as she forced one eye to open. "What happened?"

The lantern on the desk now burned, flooding the room in soft light. Worry clouded Evan's eyes. He pushed her hair away from her face. "I hoped you could tell me."

She frowned. "My head hurts."

"Did you fall and hit it?" Evan asked.

Alayna closed her eyes again, squeezing them

shut as she tried to remember. "I think someone hit me from behind."

"Did you see them?" Evan asked, still rubbing her cold hands to warm them up.

"Someone tried to get into the lodge. I followed their footsteps here." She sat straight up, ignoring the dizziness that caught her by surprise. Wrapping her arms around Evan for support, she glanced around. "Where's my gun?"

"It's right here." Evan pointed by her side, his breath warm on her cold cheek.

Alayna sighed, more from his presence than locating her firearm. "Oh, thank goodness. I'd have hated to explain that one."

Evan pulled her a little closer, resting his chin on her hair. "You're so cold, you're shaking. You really had me worried. When I returned to the lobby, the front door was wide open, but you didn't answer me when I called out."

"How did you find me then?" She rubbed at the sore place on her head, happy there wasn't any blood. "Thank you for that, by the way."

He laughed softly against her hair, sending little sparks all through her. "When I ran out on the porch, I saw the fresh footprints in the snow. Whoever it was must have hit you and run. I heard a door slam at the other end when I entered the barn. I thought the wind did it, but it could have been the perp."

"What's going on here, Evan?" Alayna motioned to the bed across the room. "Two bodies, the bear, and now someone whacked me over the head."

"I wish I knew." He set her hands down on her lap. "I'm going to check to see if there's blood. Just stay still, okay?"

"Okay. But I didn't feel anything." She sat quietly as Evan gently ran his fingers through her hair and over the surface of her scalp. When he hit a particularly tender spot, she whimpered. "Ouch. That's the spot."

He nodded. "You've got a decent sized lump there, but I don't think you're bleeding."

"We need to get back to the lodge." She tried to stand but wobbled some. The barn floor shifted. Or maybe she shifted. Evan caught her as she stumbled forward.

"Whoa there, sweetheart. Maybe we ought to take things a little slower." He held her to his chest. Her face buried in the space between his shoulder and neck, she could smell the earthy scent of his soap. She breathed in deep, enjoying the feel of his touch. She hadn't realized until that moment how much she really missed being in a man's arms.

Evan had a gentle touch. Gentle but firm. Exactly how she thought a man should be. Staying right there, in his arms, indefinitely would have made her the happiest woman in the world. It definitely made her feel safe.

"We should get back inside. Marge needs to know she has a squatter, and I need to get you warm."

Imagining all the ways Evan Marshall could warm her up, Alayna placed her hands to his chest and pushed away gently. She needed to reestablish her walls before she made a poor choice for her heart. "You're right. I'm good now. Thanks for catching me."

He pressed a light kiss to her forehead. Her knees went a little weak with the slight touch. So much for erecting walls. "Anytime. Just don't disappear on me like that again. I didn't like the feeling of losing you."

"I'll try not to." Alayna took his hand and led him from the little office before he could say or do anything else. Truth be told, she liked that he'd been worried about her. Maybe a little too much. It felt good to have someone care about her again.

Together they trudged through the snow back to the lodge. The snowfall had tapered off considerably, but the wind still whipped around them, making her already sore head ache even more. Every so often,

Evan's injured foot slipped, causing him to grimace. When they finally made it to the lodge, Marge stood on the porch, wrapped in an oversized wool blanket, looking panicked.

"Where have you two been? I heard a loud bang, and when I came downstairs, I couldn't find either one of you." Her worry caused her usually smooth skin to show deep lines as she waved them inside. "Alayna! Where's your coat? You must be half frozen to death."

"I ran out of the lodge without it. It was stupid, I know."

Following the older woman inside, Evan's arm around her waist for support, Alayna had the sudden urge to curl up and sleep until June.

"Take her to the couch in front of the fireplace. The heat of the fire will warm her quickly." Marge shooed them toward the sofa they'd sat on together earlier in the evening.

Evan scooped her up, stumbling briefly with his injured leg.

"Put me down, Evan. I don't want you to hurt yourself."

He shook his head and carried her to the couch, gently placing her on the soft cushions. They seemed to be spending a lot of time on that sofa. Not that she minded.

"I can walk, you know." Alayna frowned as he pulled a large blanket over her.

He grinned and winked. "Yeah, I just wanted to see how you felt in my arms."

"What's the verdict?" Alayna asked.

"It's something I could definitely get used to."

She looked away as she felt the warmth grow in her cold cheeks. It was something she could get used to also, and that made her feel exposed and a little bit scared. "You need to lock the front door."

He gave her a long look before nodding. "Right."

Now, why did she go and say something so dumb? Alayna sighed as she watched him walk away. Evan's feelings were obviously hurt. She always said and did the wrong thing.

APPARENTLY, HIS FLIRTING GAME HAD RUSTED UP pretty badly in the last ten years or so. Alayna had looked like a deer caught in the headlights of his Jeep when he'd joked about getting used to holding her in his arms.

"Stupid fool," he muttered as he turned the

locks on the main entrance. He'd been so worried about Alayna, he'd missed that important little detail.

"Are you okay?" Marge appeared beside him holding three mugs. She offered him one.

"Thank you." He accepted the mug. "Why do you ask?"

"You're mumbling to yourself." She smiled and took a sip. "Try the tea. It's delicious."

Evan did as she said, despite his coffee preference. The taste surprised him. "This is really good."

"Do you want to tell me what happened?" Marge sipped her tea as she studied him.

"There was a loud bang in the kitchen, like you said. When I went to check on it, someone tried to get in the front door. Alayna went after them, and I found her in the barn."

"Wow. All that happened?" She looked surprised.

He nodded. "Yeah. And, Marge? You have a nonpaying guest staying in the barn."

"I have what?"

"The room where I found Alayna has a cot with a blanket and some other things that indicate someone is staying there. A squatter."

"What in the name of St. Valentine is going on around here?" She sighed. "It could be Henry."

He shook his head. "I just don't know, Marge. But don't worry, we'll figure it out."

Marge held out the third mug. "This one is for Miss Alayna. Can you deliver?"

He took the drink. "You sure you don't want to check on her?"

Marge smiled and winked at him. "I am confident she is in good hands."

"If you say so." He glanced over at the woman on the couch.

Marge lifted her mug and nudged him lightly with her elbow. "Go on, before her tea gets cold. Keep an eye on her tonight."

"Will do. I don't like that lump on the back of her head at all."

"My mama used to say that it's better for a lump to go out than in." Marge blessed herself with the sign of the cross. "God rest Mama's soul. Good night, young man. Thank you for keeping an eye on things."

Marge left him standing alone with a mug of tea in each hand. He walked over and handed one to Alayna.

"Marge?" Smiling, she took the mug.

Evan sat on the hearth, facing her. "Yeah. She says it will make you feel better."

"Of course. Tea is the answer to everything." Alayna laughed, then grimaced. "Ouch. That made my head ache."

"I'll go get you something for that in a minute. I have some meds in my room." He pointed to his foot. "I have plenty, you know, just in case. I could use a little pain relief myself right now."

"Thanks. I'd appreciate that. I don't know how you manage to walk in the snow with that thing on your leg."

"Eh, I hardly notice it anymore. Except for the fact that it's not very warm."

"Thank you for coming to find me." Alayna's gaze switched from the fire to him. "I really didn't have it on my to-do list to freeze to death today."

The light of the fire reflected in the darkness of her eyes, drawing him in.

"I'm just glad I found you." He took a sip of his tea, unable to speak anymore without his voice giving him away. The truth of the matter had been made perfectly clear to him—Alayna Baron was someone he wanted to know better.

They sat in silence for a long while, drinking their tea. Evan stoked the fire and added another log, then moved to the couch. He lifted Alayna's feet and legs and sat down, setting them back on his lap. She let him but didn't say anything.

"Can we talk about you rushing out into a storm after a possible murderer?"

Alayna frowned. "Evan—"

He held up a hand. "Don't tell me it's none of my business."

"I wasn't going to." She took a sip of her tea. "I just wanted to say that there wasn't time. The door handles shook; I called out and then ran after the perp."

"Without backup." He watched the flames dance in a little gust of wind that came down the chimney, his hands resting on Alayna's shins. She shivered slightly. He couldn't help but wonder if it was his touch or the chill in the air.

"I'm a trained professional, same as you." She shrugged. "Besides, I knew you'd find me."

Her words squeezed at his heart. "A wild snow-storm couldn't have stopped me." He reached over and picked up her hand. "Your fingers are freezing again."

"Still. They haven't warmed up yet." She wrapped both of her hands around the warm mug. "I think I've been some level of cold since the day I arrived on this mountain. Isn't the bigger issue here who's been sleeping in the barn? Is there actually a murderer running around the mountain? And did they just try to break in and kill someone else?"

Evan chuckled. "Technically, that's three questions."

"All important ones, don't you think?" Alayna stuck her tongue out at him. "You can be infuriating sometimes."

He shrugged. "Yeah, but I think I'm growing on you."

"Maybe a little." She shifted, putting her feet on the floor. "I think I'm going to go to bed for a bit. Maybe wrapping up in the blankets will help. I am literally still chilled to the bone."

Evan got up and offered her a hand. "Careful now, that lump on the ol' noggin might make you dizzy."

Thankfully, Alayna let him assist her. She stumbled a tiny bit as they moved away from the couch. "Oh, yeah. A little dizzy for sure." She took another step, losing her footing completely this time. "Wow."

Evan caught her in his arms. "Steady now," he whispered against her ear.

Alayna wrapped her arms around his waist. "I'm good now."

He pressed a kiss to her temple. "Me too. How is

it we've just met and yet I feel like I've known you forever?"

She shook her head against his chest. "I don't know, but I feel the same. Like this whole weekend was somehow meant to be. You know, except the deaths and the near break-in, of course."

Evan rubbed his hands in small circles around her back. "We should probably get you that medicine and hot shower now."

"I suppose." She sighed, leaning into him just a little more. He'd be lying if he said he didn't like the feel of her in his arms.

Evan stepped back and turned her toward the stairs. "We have no way of knowing if you hurt anything else on your way to the ground after the perp hit you on the head. Your muscles will tighten up, especially after being so cold."

"Okay, fine." She let him lead her across the lobby, his arm wrapped around her waist. "I have meds in my room. You don't need to get me any."

They took the stairs slowly as her balance still felt a little bit off. Evan kept an arm wrapped around her waist as they moved.

When they finally reached her room, Alayna unlocked her door and walked in. Evan followed her, lingering in the doorway. He looked worried.

"I'm fine." She smiled at him. "Really. I just need sleep."

He reached for her, pulling her in close enough to give her a light kiss on the lips. "You scared me tonight."

"I'm sorry I ran off like that. I can be… impulsive."

Evan's blue eyes darkened to that stormy blue she'd come to like so much. Her heartbeat kicked into high gear as he stared down at her. "No more crazy risks, okay?"

She nodded. "Okay."

"Good night, Alayna. I'll see you for breakfast?"

He looked so hopeful, it sent her heart into high gear again. "Absolutely."

Evan stepped back into the hall, pulling the door closed with him. His heart wanted to sit in a chair and keep an eye on her the rest of the night. Just to make sure she woke up again in the morning.

CHAPTER TWELVE

After standing in the hall for a full five minutes staring at her room, Evan lay in bed for a long time. Sleep eluded him as he replayed the images of the evening. Finding Alayna lying on the floor of the barn like that had awakened way too many memories. He'd barely begun to explore the feelings he had been experiencing, and the thought of losing all that so quickly had him in a real tailspin.

Knowing she was okay helped, but it still had his thoughts reeling. Christine and Daniel had died ten years ago. Could he move on and maybe give his heart to another woman?

His body sure wanted to move on. The moments of contact between them, especially the brief kiss they'd shared, had every cell in his body anxious and primed for more.

But they'd only really known each other a couple of days. Maybe he was putting the cart before the horse, as his grandad used to say. Alayna seemed to like him too, but hell, they were locked in a mountaintop lodge during a snowstorm with a potential murderer running around. It could be the constant apprehension of what might happen next driving them together.

They'd worked in the same city for who knew how long, and they'd only crossed paths once. He remembered that day very clearly now. The pain in his foot, the adrenaline rushing through him as Alayna yanked that boy off the ground, and the big, brown, expressive eyes that had caught his attention the moment she'd made eye contact. What were the chances they'd be thrown together six weeks later at a singles' retreat a couple hundred miles from Virginia Beach? During a snowstorm. With crazy things happening.

Either the universe had a plan or karma liked to play practical jokes. His vote—and his hope—went to the former.

He finally dozed off as the sky began to lighten off to the east. He tossed and turned, memories of

Christine dying mixed with nightmares of Alayna being murdered by some psycho killer. When his alarm went off, he awoke emotionally drained and physically exhausted.

After a quick shower, he dressed and crossed the hall to Alayna's room. She pulled the door open just as he raised his hand to knock.

She met him with a big smile. "Good morning, Detective."

"Good morning, PO Baron. You look so much better this morning."

She frowned. "Gee, thanks. I think."

He pressed his palm lightly to the smooth skin of her cheek. "I meant, your eyes are sparkling and your cheeks are rosy again."

Alayna laughed. "Just how old are you, anyway? That's something my foster dad would have said— my cheeks are *rosy?*"

Unable to resist the need to hold her, he wrapped his arms around her and pulled her in close. "You gave me quite the scare. It's just good to see you looking like yourself again."

Alayna rested against his chest, and he was reminded of the random thought he'd had when he'd first found her stranded on the side of the road. She fit perfectly in his arms for dancing.

And other things.

His stomach let out a loud growl, making him laugh and effectively ending the moment. "I guess it's time we go eat."

She stepped out of his arms and rubbed her own abdomen. "That's actually what woke me up. My ravenous hunger."

When they gathered the food they wanted, they took it to the game room to escape the crowds. Evan wanted a chance to discuss the things that had happened so far without others overhearing. The guests didn't know about Frank or Alayna's whack to the head, and he wanted to keep it that way.

They found a little bistro table by one of the windows. Evan pulled a chair out for Alayna.

"Why, thank you, sir." She sat down, placing her breakfast on the table in front of her.

"You're very welcome." He sat across from her, setting his own selections out on the table as well.

Alayna took a big bite out of an apple. "Mmm, this is so good."

Evan dumped a container of Greek yogurt into a bowl of granola. "I can't remember the last time I had so many meals in a row without fast food wrappers involved."

She raised an eyebrow. "You better watch it, or

you'll become so stooped and crotchety from malnutrition you'll have to collect tolls under one of the bridges."

He laughed. "You calling me a troll?"

Alayna shrugged. "Not yet." She popped a donut hole in her mouth and gave him an innocent look.

"Christine was a lot like you." Evan took a sip of his milk.

"Your wife?"

He nodded. "Yeah. High school sweetheart too. We married right after graduation. She got pregnant a few months later."

"I can't begin to imagine how that must have hurt you."

He looked over at her, surprised to see the genuine sadness in her eyes. "It was a long time ago."

"But it obviously still hurts."

A single tear escaped his right eye. He brushed it away. "After they died, I left Staunton and moved to Virginia Beach. I worked at a grocery store until I got accepted into the police academy."

"You left your family when you needed them the most?"

He turned his attention back to the snowy scene outside. "I needed space. I couldn't breathe in

Staunton. Everything and everywhere reminded me of them."

"The ocean is good for healing the soul."

He nodded slightly. "I suppose so."

"No, Henry! How do you know anything about that?" Marge entered the room with a cordless phone to her ear, a frantic expression on her face and one hand waving wildly in the air.

He sent a questioning look to Alayna, who shrugged, and then turned back to Marge.

"This was my daddy's lodge. You have no right to any of it!" Marge slammed her hand down on a table. "Stay away from my property!"

She turned the phone off and threw it across the room. It broke into several pieces. She stood there, shaking, with tears pouring down her face.

Evan stood and walked over to her. "What is it, Marge?"

Alayna went and picked up the phone. She brought the pieces over to where Marge had sat down on a chair. "Are you okay?"

Marge took the parts of the phone from Alayna and dropped them in the pocket of her cardigan. "That was just my soon-to-be ex-husband." She laid her head down on her arm on the table. "He said he heard people been dyin' up here. I demanded to know how he knew."

Evan exchanged a look with Alayna. How *did* he know?

"Said he heard it in town from one of the police officers." She let out a single sob. "He said no one will ever want to stay here if they know people are getting murdered on vacation."

"It's okay, Marge." Alayna wrapped an arm around the older woman's shoulders.

"No." She looked up at them with tearstained cheeks. "It's not okay. The judge wants me to give half the business to Henry, and I won't do it." She pounded a fist on her thigh. "I won't! This was my daddy's business."

"I'm not sure if there is anything that can be done, but we will help you if we can," Alayna said.

Marge took them each by the hand. "I appreciate your offering, but I just don't know what you can do. The law is pretty clear. I'd just hoped Henry would have been a bigger person and left my lodge alone." She stood up and smoothed down her skirt. "Please don't pay this old lady any mind. I'll be fine. Henry always gets me all worked up. It's part of the reason we are getting divorced. I need to see to some things now, if you'll excuse me."

She left the room in a rush.

"Is it normal police practice for a chief to talk about investigations to random people?" Alayna asked Evan. "I mean, maybe things are different in small towns?"

He shook his head. "Yeah, I don't think so. Something else is going on here."

"I think so too."

Evan sat down at the table. "We need to go back to the barn and search that office." His stomach made a gurgling sound. "But first we finish breakfast."

"Okay." Alayna sat down again as well, taking another bite of her apple.

"I swear it's even colder today than last night." Alayna pulled her hat down further over her ears as her breath came out in little puffs.

The snow had taken on the appearance of millions of sparkling diamonds as the icy flakes on the ground caught the pale sunlight. The branches of the tall pines hung heavy, showcasing the white clouds of snow they'd collected during the storm.

Evan pulled the zipper up on his jacket and

rubbed his gloved hands together. "At least the snow stopped. The wind is cold enough without all that ice water slapping us in the face." He reached up and tugged the fuzzy pom-pom on her hat. "This is something I haven't seen since I was a kid."

"Hey! Leave my puff ball alone." Alayna swatted at his hand. "It's soft, fluffy, and my favorite color. If you don't like it...." She held her hands in a fighting pose.

He raised his own hands in surrender, laughing. "I love it! I swear!"

"Whatever." She huffed as she climbed down the stone steps. "These are pretty icy. Be careful with that fancy footwear of yours."

They trudged through the hard snow, following the footprints they'd made the night before. The crunch of their steps coupled with the awkwardness of Evan's gait echoed through the otherwise quiet land. Even the strong winds seemed to have moved on. They only encountered a gust or two as they walked. His exposed skin burned in the cold air.

She inhaled deeply. "Can't you just smell the cold?"

Evan tried sniffing too but ended up snorting. "Sorry. My snot is so frozen, I can't smell anything."

When they reached the barn, she held a finger to

her lips and motioned to what looked like fresh tracks in the snow blown inside the barn doors. They were too big to be hers and too even to be Evan's. They had the wide tread of a work boot or snow boot, which neither of them had anyway.

They stepped inside, careful not to creak the broken door and alert the squatter to their presence. A musty scent filled the dim space. A pile of hay bales she hadn't noticed the night before sat just inside the door to their left. Alayna led the way to the office. Standing off to the side, she peeked around the doorframe. The room appeared to be empty, but it had the night before as well, making her extra cautious this time.

She stepped inside the small space with Evan close behind her. Together, they scanned the room, but there was no one there.

Alayna pointed across the room. "The cot is gone."

"What?" Evan looked where she pointed.

"The cot that was there last night with the blanket and pillow. Gone. The lantern too."

"Well, I'll be damned." All they could see were some marks in the dirty floor where the makeshift bed had been set up. Evan crossed the room to the spot in question. "They sure did leave in a hurry, whoever it was." He leaned down beside the desk and picked something up. He turned around, disgust on his face and something held between two gloved fingers. "They left behind their jockey shorts."

"Ewww." Alayna laughed. "How does one run off and leave their underwear behind?"

"I think he'd have noticed in this cold." Evan tossed the garment onto the desk. "Let's see if he forgot anything else."

She pulled open a drawer on the desk. A penny, a paperclip, and a carpenter's pencil were all it held. The other two drawers in the desk proved to be empty, as well as the single cabinet in the room.

Evan leaned against the desk, resting his hands on the edge and taking the weight off his injured foot. "Well, this place is a bust. Whoever was here must have run after you discovered their hiding spot."

She kicked at a dust bunny on the floor. "It definitely looks that way."

"I'm thinking it was a homeless person, maybe someone who lives off the trails along the parkway, looking to get out of the snow and cold."

Alayna frowned. "So, why not stay *inside* the lodge?"

"I have no idea. No money, maybe."

A loud slam sounded through the old barn, making her jump. "What was that?"

"Sounded like one of the doors blowing in the wind." Evan walked out of the office and looked around. "The door we came through is now definitely closed."

The only light came from a couple of windows high up over the loft, but it barely took the edge off the darkness.

Her nostrils burned a little. Something wasn't right. "Do you smell that?" She turned in a full circle, scanning the barn, but saw nothing that fit the acrid scent.

Evan sniffed. "Dust and dirt? Yeah."

"No, it's something else." Alayna jogged over to the door and pushed at the latch. It didn't budge. Using all her weight against the door made no difference—it still wouldn't move. "Evan. I think we're in trouble."

"What's wrong?" He stepped in beside her.

Alayna breathed in. "Don't you smell that?"

He took a deep breath. "Gas."

She nodded. "Yeah."

Tiny tendrils of smoke began to slip in under the doors and swirl around his legs. "Alayna? I think we have a real problem here." He motioned to the smoke.

"We need to get out of here, Evan." She ran across the barn to the other door and threw herself at it. The impact tossed her to the ground.

"Alayna! Are you okay?" Evan ran awkwardly toward her as smoke began to seep in under that door also.

"I'm fine! But we're in serious trouble." She jumped to her feet. "Come on! We need to find a way out of here. This old wood is going to go up like paper."

"The snow has the wood pretty wet. It should slow things down," Evan said. "Still, we need to find a way out of here."

They ran to each of the closed off rooms and shoved open the doors, looking for some way out but found nothing. The air became stuffy as the wood structure burned. Her eyes stung and her lungs ached.

"Why aren't there any low windows in this place?" Alayna stood in the middle of the building as smoke thickened and swirled with the drafts coming between the wall planks.

"Pull your collar up over your nose and mouth. It should help a little." Evan coughed as he dug through a pile of random items, tossing things aside until he pulled out a piece of a lawn mower blade. "Don't worry; I've got an idea." He felt along the wall until he found a place that satisfied him. "The wood isn't warm here yet. Come help me."

Both doors were fully aflame now, and the fire had spread to the walls, burning fairly quickly. The smoke grew even thicker, making it near impossible to breathe. "What are you doing?"

"I'm going to use this blade to pry away some of the boards." He shoved the edge of the steel into a space between two boards and put his weight into it. They heard a slight creak. He shifted the steel up a few inches and repeated the process. The smoke burned her lungs as she coughed.

Over the rush of the flames, she could hear loud voices outside the barn calling for help.

"Did you know that fire burns up?" Alayna coughed again as they worked on the wall boards.

"Yes, why?" Evan grunted as he shoved the blade deep in between two planks and used it like a crowbar.

Alayna pointed up as sweat began to drip from her forehead and run into her eyes. The fire had climbed one wall all the way to the rafters, heating the air inside the barn to uncomfortable temperatures. Flames licked at the old wood, stoking the fire. "It's really going up fast."

Evan shoved again, popping one of the boards loose. "I'm through! Here, help me pull this one out!"

Alayna grabbed the piece of wood near the bottom. She yanked her hand away as smoke snaked into the space. "Ouch! It's hot!"

"We've got to get out of here!" Evan pried at the board with the old blade, freeing it from the wall. He threw it past them to the floor. Flames licked at the bottom of the opening. The smoke in the barn swirled around them as it was sucked out through the gap Evan had made.

Her fingers burned, and her lungs ached from the acrid air. Sweat poured from her face and soaked through the shirt under her sweater. A loud groan overhead caught their attention. "Look!" Alayna pointed at one of the beams. It burned in a steady flame where it met the wall of the barn.

Evan yanked at another board, adjacent to the first. It pulled loose with a hard tug, sending him to the floor. "Evan!" Alayna grabbed at his hands, pulling him to his feet and stumbling backward into the burning wall. "Are you okay?"

"I'm fine." He yanked her away from the fire. "Can you get through that space okay without getting burned?' He motioned to the opening he created. Little tongues of flames licked at the bottom of the next plank.

"I can." Without waiting for instructions, Alayna jumped over the flames and out into the snow, landing facedown in the white stuff. Fresh air rushed into her lungs, setting off a loud coughing fit. Evan tumbled to the ground beside her. She rolled over onto her back and looked up at the barn, now almost completely consumed in flames. She'd landed on her wrist wrong, but otherwise she seemed okay.

Evan pulled himself up, then wrapped his arms around her chest, dragging her away from the fire. When they were clear of the intense heat, he dropped to his knees beside her. "Are you okay, Alayna?" His eyes had that hurricane-ravaged ocean appearance again as fear and worry drained his features of any color.

"I twisted my wrist up good, but everything else is still where it should be."

"Thank God." He gently swiped some snow from her face and off her eyelashes with his gloved thumb.

"Hey!" someone yelled. "Over here! There were people in there!"

Evan ran his hands up and down her arms,

around her back and over her face and head. "Are you sure you aren't hurt?"

She shivered, as much from the sensations his touch caused as from the cold. "You worry too much."

He pressed tiny kisses across her forehead, cheeks, and nose. "I was terrified I'd lose you before I ever had the chance to really know you."

Alayna let out a little sigh as she ran her fingers over his hair and down his neck. She let her fingers run along the line of his chin and stroke lightly through the stubble on his face. "You aren't the only one that was afraid. The way you fell, I thought you'd hit your head again."

"Oh no! *No!*" They heard Marge's cries over the roar of the flames.

"Marge," Alayna said. "That poor woman."

Evan stood up once more, carefully pulling her to her feet as well. They made their way over to the front of the burning barn to find Marge on her knees in the snow, tears running down her face.

Guests had gathered on the snow-covered lawn and front porch of the lodge, pointing and looking shocked. Large, black smoke plumes churned high into the air over the burning structure.

Marge spotted them and jumped to her feet. "Evan! Alayna! What happened? Did you see?"

"No," Evan replied. "But someone set that fire intentionally. They locked us in the barn first."

"You were in the barn?" Marge's eyes opened wide as she seemed to fully take in their appearance. She took Alayna's face in her hands. "Are you both okay?"

Alayna nodded. "We barely made it out. Evan found an old lawn mower blade and used it to pry away some boards."

A loud, gut-churning groan filled the sky as the roof to the structure collapsed. Everyone looked up and watched as a cloud of embers rose up into the air and dropped in a shower all around them.

"We need to get back!" Alayna led Marge toward the lodge as Evan started pacing the area, looking up at the lodge. No fire truck would get to them anytime soon, so they just had to keep an eye on the lodge to be sure the embers didn't reach the log and stone building.

Marge wrung her hands as she leaned into Alayna. "Why? Why is all this happening?"

She hugged Marge. "I wish I knew."

"Once Henry hears about this, he's going to try even harder to ruin my business. I mean, it's just an old barn, but I'd hoped to bring horses back in the spring. Maybe offer riding lessons and trail rides."

Alayna frowned. "Did Henry know this?"

Marge shrugged. "We'd talked about it in the past."

"Maybe we should go inside?" Alayna asked. "It might be easier not to watch, and you must be freezing without a heavy coat on. Evan is keeping an eye on the lodge."

Marge sniffed and wiped her eyes with the sleeve of her sweater. "No. I need to see it. To make it real. First, Daddy's bear. Then Haley and Frank. And you, last night. Now this."

"I don't think what happened last night was related to the others. The fire either. Evan and I think you may have had a squatter in the barn who got mad that we ruined his good thing."

Marge turned to look at her. "So he burns my barn to the ground?"

Alayna shrugged. "I honestly don't know, Marge. I wish I had all the answers for you. I really do. Evan may have a better idea. He's a detective; his mind works a certain way that mine doesn't. I'm sure he will talk it through with you later though, if you like."

She nodded. "Evan is a good boy. Reminds me of my own son."

"Marge? You have a son? I had no idea."

"He lives in California. He's—" The rest of her reply was drowned out by the rush of noise as two of the barn walls fell into the fire. More embers flew up into the air at the same time as a gust of wind kicked up, whipping the burning bits all over the place. Guests squealed and screamed as the hot wood landed on their bodies and the stone porch they stood on. Smoke started to grow above their head.

Alayna looked up to see a piece of the barn settle on one of the wood rafters and start to smolder. "Marge! Do you have a fire extinguisher?"

The other woman looked up, saw the fire trying to start, and ran off. The front door whipped open just as she reached for the handle, knocking her to the ground. Jed ran out with a large extinguisher, white foam coming out of the nozzle.

As soon as he was confident the fire had gone out, Jed ran back to where Marge still sat on the stone floor. "Ms. Marge! I'm so sorry. I didn't hurt you, did I?"

He scooped her up off the floor and set her on her feet. "I'm fine, Jed. Just a little shaken up. Thank you for saving the lodge."

"All I did was squash a little smoker."

She smiled at the young man and pressed her palm to his cheek. "Where there's smoke, there soon will be fire. Thank you for saving my home."

"Aw, Ms. Marge. I'd always help you." He motioned toward the fire that had begun to slow. "What happened, anyway? I was out in the woods taking a walk when I smelled the smoke. The lodge looked fine, so I thought it was the fireplace. When I came in the kitchen door, I heard everyone running out the front door."

Alayna heard this and interjected. "You were taking a walk in below freezing temperatures?"

Jed turned to look at her, his eyes narrowed. "Yeah. Why not? I got warm clothes."

She raised an eyebrow. "Just seems a little odd to me."

"Everything okay up there?" Evan called from the yard.

She gave him a thumbs-up. "We're good. Jed brought out a fire extinguisher."

He returned the thumbs-up and went back to pacing around the lodge.

"The fire seems to be burning down," Marge said.

As she spoke, the skeletons of the remaining two walls collapsed, sending a fresh ember shower into the air. Without a wind gust though, most of them just fell back onto the pile of burning wood. Thankfully.

Other guests began to filter back into the lodge when it became obvious it wasn't going to burn as well.

Marge left Jed and walked over to the porch rail. "It's a good thing the tin roof is covered in snow. Double protection from the embers."

Evan climbed the steps, gripping the rail and moving slowly. "I think the lodge is out of danger now."

"My dear, you must be exhausted." Marge took him by the arm and patted the back of his hand. "And hungry. Come inside, I'll get you some chocolate chip cookies and milk."

Alayna watched as Marge took Evan into the lodge, a tiny twinge of envy poking at her. Marge appeared old enough to be Evan's mother, so there really wasn't any reason to be jealous. She'd mentioned to Alayna earlier that Evan reminded her of her son. Her curiosity had certainly been aroused.

As soon as Alayna was alone on the porch, she let out a long breath. The last of the fire crackled quietly, the sound disturbing the stillness that had settled in around her. Little piles of ash dotted the once pristine landscape, marring the beauty of the mountain in so many ways.

The events of the last two days had her mind in complete overdrive. When Maddy had sent her off on a mountain getaway, she'd fully planned to spend the four days reading and avoiding the other guests. This had become the furthest thing from a quiet weekend escape.

Of course, if she hadn't made the trip, she may not have crossed paths with Evan again. And if she was being completely honest, that was a definite perk to being stranded on a mountain. Even if there might be a killer stranded there too.

CHAPTER THIRTEEN

THE COLD FINALLY GETTING TO HER, ALAYNA WENT inside the lodge and up to her room without stopping to look for Evan. She needed a minute to herself to even think about processing what had happened that day. Or heck, over the last forty-eight hours or so. After taking off her coat and kicking off her boots, she flopped on the bed and lay there, spread eagle and facedown. The colorful quilt had several threadbare spots that hadn't been visible until she got up close and personal with them. The tiny stitches combining the multicolored pieces of fabric were perfectly placed. She traced a couple with her fingertip.

Her mom had had several hand-sewn quilts made by Grandma Baron. She remembered studying the different patterns intently as a little kid. No one seemed to know who had taken them after her parents died though. If only they hadn't gone through and sold everything before she had the chance to really look around and keep a few things. The powers that be thought she'd rather have a nice big bank account when she turned eighteen instead of keepsakes of her childhood.

A loud rap on the door had her jumping up off the bed.

"Alayna? Are you in there?"

Evan. Darn it.

She reluctantly pulled the door open to find him holding a glass of milk and a plate of cookies that smelled heavenly. "You really like those cookies, don't you?"

"More than life itself." Evan grinned and handed them to her. "Marge sent all this up to you."

Alayna rubbed her hands together before accepting the snack. "Yum. Thank you for delivering."

His expression turned serious. "Are you okay, Alayna?"

"Fine. Why?" She knew why. She just hadn't begun to face reality yet, preferring to live in denial for a bit longer instead.

Evan frowned. "You didn't come find us when you came in. I got worried when you weren't outside."

"I'm a big girl, Evan. I didn't think I had to check in with you."

He placed his hands on her shoulders and looked into her eyes. The blue of his eyes had already begun to reflect his mood, like one of those mood rings she'd played with as a kid. "Someone tried to kill us, remember?"

Well, that ruined her plan to totally ignore the obvious. She sighed. "Yes, I remember. And I'm fine."

He stepped inside and closed the door behind him. "It's okay to *not* be fine."

She walked over and set her glass and plate on the little table. "I really am fine. I'm not hurt. You got us out of the barn. We need to focus now on finding out who wanted *us* dead. Is it the same person that killed the others?"

Evan exhaled heavily, his frustration obvious to her. "Just promise me that if you need to talk about it, you will. I'm here for you."

Knowing she should feel bad for it, she kind of enjoyed watching his eyes darken to the color of storm clouds again.

"Are you some kind of expert on narrowly

escaping death?" She took a bite of a cookie. "Marge really makes the best cookies."

Evan laughed. "Smooth subject change."

"What? These are amazing." Alayna took a swallow of milk. "And I promise, if I need to talk, I will let you know. Okay?"

She saw the visible relief in his features as his eyes returned to their usual crystal blue.

"Good." He stepped in close and used his forefinger to lift her chin, so she had to meet his gaze. "I am only across the hall if you need me. Anytime, day or night. Okay?"

She nodded, mouth full of cookie.

"I'm going to go downstairs and talk to Marge again. I can't shake the feeling that all of this business has something to do with her husband trying to take the lodge from her." He picked up a piece of one of her cookies and shoved it in his mouth. She thought about smacking it out of his hand, but that would have ended up in wasted goodness. Instead, she snatched the plate up and walked across the room. Evan chuckled. She'd made her point.

Alayna sipped her milk. "See if you can find out if Jed usually takes walks in the woods in nut-freezing cold."

Evan laughed so hard, cookie crumbs flew out of

his mouth. "Nut-freezing cold! What would you know about that?"

"What? I had a foster brother."

He shook his head, still smiling. "You are one of a kind, Alayna."

"Yeah and don't you forget it." She set the plate and glass down on a small table.

"Why do you want to know about Jed?"

Alayna sat down in a chair by a window. "When he came tearing out of the lodge with the fire extinguisher, he said he'd been walking in the woods when he smelled the smoke. I still don't get why anyone would *choose* to be outside." She motioned to the window, rubbing her hands up and down her arms. "It's just way too cold for that."

EVAN PERCHED ON THE EDGE OF HER BED, GRINNING. "Some people like this kind of weather, you know. I used to."

"But then you wised up and moved to the beach."

"Yeah, I guess." His expression turned serious. "I could have sworn I saw Jed in the kitchen when we left this morning."

She shrugged. "When he came running outside,

he had on a coat and work boots, so it's possible he'd left after we did. I just don't know why anyone would choose to go outside right now if they don't have to." Shivering for effect, Alayna rubbed her palms together.

Shaking his head, Evan gave her a teasing smile. "You were born and raised a beach girl, weren't you?"

"Absolutely."

"Well, us mountain dwellers actually like the snow and enjoy outdoor activities in the winter." He pointed to himself. "Me. I'm one of those mountain dwellers. There's nothing like skiing or snow-boarding after a fresh snowfall."

"When was the last time you were home to visit?" Alayna asked, just before taking a bite of another cookie.

"When my brother Adam got engaged about five months ago."

She looked confused. "You drove all the way from Virginia Beach because your brother got engaged?"

Evan laughed. "That's what Marshalls do. We love a good excuse for a party."

"Marge has a son."

Now that was unexpected news. "She does? How do you know?"

"She mentioned it outside. She said you remind her of him."

Interesting tidbit of information. He stood up. "Marge is a woman of many mysteries. I'm going to go downstairs to talk to her and check the fire. It should have burnt itself out by now, but I don't want to take any chances with the lodge."

Alayna nodded. "It's sheer luck it didn't ignite half the mountain. When do you think the road will be open again? That barn is a suspected crime scene, technically."

"I'm going to put in a call to the police department as soon as I get downstairs. The one good thing about old-style wall phones—you don't need electricity to make them run like a cordless one." Evan walked over to the door but stopped with his hand on the knob and turned to look at her. "Call down to the front desk if you need me."

"I'm fine, Evan. Really. I am." She waved him off. "Now go. Leave me alone with this plate of deliciousness. We need our privacy."

Evan laughed to himself all the way down the stairs to the first floor. Now that Alayna had begun to loosen up, he liked her sense of humor and her quick, sometimes sarcastic wit. She had so many things about her that reminded him of Christine, yet she also had a completely unique personality. Different from anyone he'd ever met before.

About halfway down the stairs, he heard someone scream. Half running and half hopping with his messed-up foot, he nearly fell the rest of the way down the steps. When he made it to the lobby, a small crowd had gathered.

"What happened?" Alayna appeared beside him. "I heard someone scream."

"I'm not sure yet." When they reached the little group, they worked their way through the people to find Marge in a heap on the ground, not moving. An empty pitcher lay in a puddle of water beside her.

"Anyone know what happened?" Alayna asked, looking around the group.

A woman about her age raised her hand. "I saw. I'm the one who screamed. Ms. Marge was filling the water dispenser when she just passed out."

Evan leaned down and pressed a finger to Marge's carotid artery, searching for a pulse.

"Do you feel anything?" Alayna asked.

He nodded, sighing in relief. "Pulse is strong. She must have fainted. Let's get her off the floor."

Evan lifted the older woman up and carried her over to the couch by the fireplace. Setting her down with her head on a pillow, he smoothed her hair back out of her face. He caught sight of Alayna watching him with an odd expression. Was that a tiny bit of the green-eyed monster showing in her brown eyes? He kind of liked that she might be a little jealous.

Gently shaking her by the shoulder, Evan tried to wake their hostess. "Marge? Are you okay? Marge. Wake up now."

"I'll get some water and a cool cloth." Alayna headed to the kitchen.

"Is she going to be all right?" asked the woman who had seen her pass out.

Marge began to stir. "She's going to be just fine, aren't you, Marge?" Evan rubbed the back of one of her hands.

"Mmm... what happened?" Marge tried to sit up, but Evan gently settled her back against the pillow.

"It looks like you fainted," he said.

"I did?" Marge looked as confused as she sounded. "Now why would I go and do something like that?

Alayna returned with a cold compress and handed it to him. "I have no idea. I was hoping you could tell us." Evan replied, placing the cool cloth on Marge's forehead.

She reached up and touched the towel. "I was

filling the water cooler when everything just sort of faded away. I can't imagine why."

"It was probably the stress of the fire and everything else."

Her eyes closed again. "Maybe. Probably. If you don't mind, I'm just going to rest here for a couple of minutes."

"I'd say that is perfectly fine." He patted her hand and then addressed the small group of guests. "Everything is under control now. No need to worry."

"I don't think anything has been under control since we got here," one of the male guests said. "I mean, that girl slips and falls and *dies*, the storm of the century traps us on this mountain, and now an entire barn burned down and no one seems the least bit bothered by it!"

Evan held up a hand to indicate he needed to stop. "I'm really sorry, sir, that this hasn't been your ideal vacation. It hasn't been mine either. But getting all worked up right now isn't going to clear that road and rebuild a barn."

The man huffed and actually stomped his foot. "This is the absolute worst vacation I have ever been on."

"It is what it is, sir. We can't change the snowstorm. You came here to meet new people, so why don't you just focus on that? It's the perfect opportunity—you have a captive audience."

Standing behind the agitated man, Alayna snort-laughed, covering her mouth with her hand to hold the rest in. The man turned and glared at her but said nothing else. He just walked away.

Marge squeezed his hand and whispered her thanks. He nodded and gave her a little squeeze back.

He motioned to Alayna to join them. "I need to call the police chief and bring him up to speed on what's been happening around here. Can you sit with Marge?"

She smiled at the other woman. "It would be my pleasure."

"I don't know how I would have managed if the two of you hadn't been here this weekend."

Alayna settled on the floor beside the couch, crossing her legs and leaning back on her hands. "Ouch!" She sat forward and cradled one arm in the other.

"Are you okay, dear?" Marge looked worried.

"I totally forgot I twisted this arm up when I fell out of the barn. It stopped hurting a while ago. I guess maybe it just doesn't want to bend that way right now."

"I'm going to go make that call now." He strode away, heading to the landline behind the reception desk. One thing that man had been right about: this certainly wasn't the vacation he'd been expecting.

CHAPTER FOURTEEN

"WHAT EXACTLY IS GOING ON UP THERE, DETECTIVE?" Chief Roman had listened quietly as he relayed the news of the fire and the barn squatter.

"I wish I knew, sir. On one hand, it feels like someone has it in for Marge, and on the other, some of it can be explained away by other causes. I mean, both deaths could have been accidental. But someone definitely whacked Alayna on the head and set the barn on fire."

The chief let out a low whistle. "My gut tells me they are all connected. The scuttlebutt around town is that they are going to clear that road out tomorrow."

"Does the department have access to a helicopter? There's plenty of landing room up here, believe it or not."

"The roof collapsed on the hangar. They're trying to dig her out. One way or another, we will get the bird in the air or the road cleared."

"The second they do, send a team. We got everything from simple assault to arson for y'all to investigate." Evan glanced over at Alayna and Marge and chuckled. "This is the first working vacation I have been on. Not too sure I like it."

Roman laughed. "Not exactly the hookup weekend you expected, is it?"

"Not at all!"

He heard a radio crackle in the background. The noise suddenly disappeared. Roman must have shut it off. "I'll give a call up there when the road is clear and let you know we're on the way. Right now, I've got a situation to tend to. Y'all take care up there. Keep those guests alive."

"Will do, Chief. See you in a day or so." Evan hung up the phone and let out a long exhale. Knowing the road would be cleared soon was good news. Now if they could just all stay safe and alive in the meantime, that would be fantastic.

Alayna still sat on the floor near Marge. Her face was animated with emotion. Wondering what they were talking about, he headed back to the fireplace. As soon as he approached, they both stopped talking.

"Was it something I did?" he said, sitting on the stone hearth and stretching out his legs. He'd had so much action the last few days, he might never walk right again.

Alayna motioned to his injured foot. "You're limping more."

He sighed. "It's been a rough few days. I've got good news though. The chief of police says they're going to work on clearing the road tomorrow."

Marge sat up and clasped her hands. "That is amazing news. I absolutely hate that Haley and Frank are still in that cellar. They both deserve so much more."

Alayna stood up and straightened her sweater. "That *is* good news. I had begun to think we'd be stuck here forever."

The wistfulness in her voice stabbed at his heart. He'd liked being with her, and he worried that once this was over, she'd go back to being closed off and he'd go back to being alone, living in the same city as strangers once more.

He didn't like that idea at all.

Marge rose, gripping the arm of the sofa as she

steadied herself. "If you all don't mind, I'm going to go and check on the meal prep. It's nothing fancy—just sandwiches and salad, but at least I can make sure it looks appetizing."

"Do you need any help, Marge?" Alayna asked.

"No, dear. Thank you. You've had quite the day already. I think you've earned a rest." Marge headed to the kitchen, leaving Evan alone with Alayna.

"It has been quite a day, hasn't it?" She walked over to the window and looked out. Little black spots dotted the snow where ash had fallen.

He came up behind her and rested his hands on her shoulders. "It definitely has been."

She turned into his arms and buried her face against his chest. "We could have died in that barn. I don't think I'm as fine as I want to think."

Evan ran his hands up and down her back in soothing little motions. "It hits you as soon as the adrenaline spike wears off."

"Ten years as a parole officer, and this is the first time I ever felt fear like that."

The scent of citrus mingled with burning wood as he breathed deeply against her hair. "I was scared too. When I heard that door slam, I got worried, but when that first whiff of smoke hit me, my heart fell straight into my stomach."

Alayna stepped back. "I keep thinking about how Jed was *taking a walk* when the barn was set on fire."

"Do you think he had something to do with the fire?" Evan hadn't really considered that fact, but now that Alayna had voiced her concern, it sort of made sense. In the worst possible way.

"It's possible." She turned back toward the window, tapping the glass lightly with her fingertip. "Probably not, though. I still can't believe it happened."

"What about the squatter that had been staying there?" He strode across the room to get a better view of the remains of the barn in relation to the wood line closest to the kitchen entrance. "I supposed he would've had time to get back in the woods before we broke out of the barn."

The lights blinked. Alayna glanced around the large lobby. "Uh-oh, the generator seems to be struggling again."

The blinking stopped. "Might just be another little hiccup in the system."

Alayna dropped onto the sofa and hugged one of the throw pillows to her chest. "No one is going to believe this story when I get back home. It feels like a game of Clue. The cook did it in the barn with a candlestick or something."

He couldn't stop his laughter. "At least it wasn't the butcher in the bathroom with the hatchet."

Alayna tossed the pillow at him. "You're making fun of me."

He laughed some more, tossing it back at her. "I am not. It was just funny."

The lights blinked once more, and then the power went out completely. A chorus of *ahs* and *what happened* filled the lodge. A minute later, Marge bustled into the room. "The generator has stopped. I need to find Jed to check it out."

"I'll go out and check on it," Evan said. "Let me just run upstairs and grab my coat."

"Oh, thank you so much, dear. If it's no trouble, I'd appreciate it. You both have been such a godsend to me through all of this."

He gave the woman his warmest smile. She reminded him so much of his mother, and after her fainting spell that morning, the last thing she needed was any more stress. "It's no trouble at all."

She turned to Alayna. "He's such a good man, don't you think? Some woman will be very lucky to scoop him up." Marge winked at Alayna and whisked away toward the dining room, blowing them each a kiss. "I need to set up the seating chart for dinner.

The two of you will have your usual table, don't worry."

"I see the stress hasn't affected her gift." Alayna set the pillow down and stood up. "I'll go with you."

He shook his head. "It's okay, I can handle it. You should stay in here where it's warm."

She looked like she wanted to argue, but a huge gust of wind slammed against the windows, making her jump. "I guess I'll do a quick check of the lodge while you're outside."

By the time he got his coat and hat from his room and headed outside, guests had begun to congregate in the lobby area again. Marge was trying to herd them into the event room for a game of bingo as he pulled the door closed behind him. Playing bingo made him think more of an assisted living center than a singles' weekend, but their options for entertainment and distraction had become limited.

The scent of charred wood hung heavy in the icy air. Smoke still rose from the pile of rubble. They were way beyond lucky that the lodge hadn't caught fire as well. If not for the tin roof, it probably would have.

Evan trudged through the snow, his injured foot beginning to ache from the cold and force of walking through the hard material. He had no idea exactly where the generator sat, so he just followed the wall until the end and turned, knowing it had to be nearby.

And then he stopped.

The generator—or what was left of it—lay in pieces in the snow. Amber liquid, gas most likely, had soaked into the snow around it. He moved closer, looking around to make sure he was alone. When he got to the machine, he sucked in a breath. It looked like someone had taken a sledgehammer to it.

Moving through the snow as best he could, he ran back into the lodge. Slamming the door behind him, he locked it and then stood there for a minute, trying to catch his breath. Alayna walked in from the event room.

"Evan! That's one exciting game of bingo. Mr. Johnson just won a game and did a cartwheel. Well, he tried anyway." She stopped talking and gave him a once over. "What happened? Are you okay?"

"The generator." His breaths were still coming in short puffs. He bent at the waist and inhaled deeply several times.

"What about it? Is it out of gas?" she asked.

He stood up and shook his head. "No. It's... destroyed. Someone destroyed it."

She rested her hands on her hips and looked at him with an expression of disbelief. "Why...? Who...?" Throwing her hands in the air, she exhaled. "I don't even know the right questions to ask anymore."

Unzipping his jacket, Evan slipped it off and did his best to knock the rest of the snow off his feet on the rug inside the door. "I don't either. I will say though that I fully expect this foot of mine to never heal. It's having a fit with me right now for running."

"Why don't you go upstairs and rest? I'll stay down here and keep an eye on things."

"I won't be long, I promise." He leaned in and gave her a quick kiss. "It's going to be dark in a bit, and with no lights, I'm going to feel like a sitting duck waiting for the next bad thing to happen."

"Hey." She gave him that warm smile he'd become so attached to. "We'll be fine. We've got two of Virginia Beach's finest on the job."

He nodded and gave her one last kiss. "I'll back soon, I promise."

"What can I do to help, Marge?" Alayna had told her about the generator. The other woman walked off quietly after hearing the news. After giving her a few minutes to process the information first, Alayna now found her in the kitchen pulling out butane lighters and a variety of jar candles from the pantry.

Marge handed her one of the lighters. "You could go light the candles on all the tables in the dining room. It's going to be dark at dinnertime."

"No problem." She took the lighter and wandered back to the dining room. The guests were in little groups around the lodge, chatting idly, but she could still feel the tension in the air. Their smiles were negated by the fear and questions in their eyes.

"Excuse me?" One of the female guests appeared beside her. "My name's Mary. You're Alayna, right?"

She nodded. "I am. What can I do for you?"

"Are you a cop?"

Mary's bluntness caught her off guard. "Not exactly."

The other woman looked at her, disbelief in her eyes. "My brother is a cop, and you and that man you spend all your time with act an awful lot like he does."

"Evan *is* a cop. I am an officer with Juvenile Services in Virginia Beach."

Her eyes lit up, and she smiled from ear to ear. "I knew it!"

Alayna held a finger to her lips. "I'm not sure Evan wants anyone to know."

Mary nodded and pulled an imaginary zipper across her lips. "Oh, of course. I know how cops can be. My lips are sealed."

"I appreciate that." She pointed to a light fixture above them. "The generator is out of commission. It's going to get dark soon. I have to finish lighting some candles for Marge."

As she began to walk away, Mary took ahold of her arm. "Something bad is happening here, isn't it?"

Alayna turned and looked at her. "What?"

"There's no way that fire started on its own." Mary's expression pretty much dared her to say otherwise.

"We won't know anything until the fire marshal and arson investigator can get up here to figure it out." She tried again to leave, but Mary just walked with her.

"Alayna, I know you are keeping something from me. From all of us. We have a right to know." Mary's accusatory tone aggravated her. Why wouldn't the other woman just let it lie?

"I don't *know* anything, Mary." She headed to the

event room. The sun had sunk pretty low in the sky. She needed to get those candles lit.

"First that girl dies. Then the barn burns down. What else aren't you saying? I can see there's something."

They entered the room by the little stage where she and Evan had done their karaoke performance. She smiled a little at the memory of Evan dipping her deeply as they finished their grand finale.

Mary wandered over to the checkers set she and Evan had been using the day before. It felt more like a lifetime ago, actually. She chattered on as Alayna finished seeking out all the candles. As she stood on tiptoe to light one on a shelf, Mary let out a little squeal.

"Mary! What's wrong?" She ran across the room to the where the other woman stood. "Are you okay?"

Mary didn't say anything; she just lifted a shaking arm and pointed behind a sofa. Alayna shifted her position so see what Mary saw and gasped.

Jed lay facedown on the floor, a pool of red liquid surrounding him. As she stepped closer, she could see the handle of the butcher knife sticking out of his back. "Not again." Alayna squatted next to Jed's body and felt for a pulse but came up empty.

"Is he... *dead*?" Mary asked.

A soft jumble of voices floated in through the door. She jumped up and clapped a hand over Mary's mouth. "Shhh! There's no need to alarm everyone."

Mary shook her head vigorously and pushed at her hand. "Everyone deserves to know. There's a killer among us!"

"Will you be quiet!" Alayna whisper-yelled. "I don't want you to scare the other guests."

"Is everything okay in here?" Marge appeared in the doorway then walked over to where Mary and Alayna stood. She clapped her hand over her mouth when she spotted the body on the floor. "Please tell me that's not Jed."

Alayna left Mary and wrapped Marge in a hug, turning her away from the body. "I'm so sorry, Marge."

The tears flowed then. Every ounce of stress and anguish from the weekend seemed to leave her all at once. "I can't take this anymore! Make him stop!"

Alayna stepped back, holding Marge at arm's length. "Make who stop what?"

She shook her head, even as the tears continued to flow. "Henry. My ex. It has to be him doing all this! I mean, I never thought he could kill someone, but I also never expected him to have a whole family back east in Emporia either."

"Your ex-husband has another family?" Alayna asked, momentarily distracted from the murder victim by a polygamous husband.

"We were married for twelve years. I met him a decade after my first husband died. I didn't think I'd ever fall in love again, but Henry swept me off my feet. He was all Prince Charming rescuing the sad, heartbroken maiden. Anyway, Henry drives long-haul trucks, so I never questioned it when he'd disappear for days at a time. He always called to check in. I thought he was on the road, when in actuality he had a wife and a family in Emporia."

"I'm so sorry, Marge. I can't even imagine what that felt like."

"Um, hello," Mary said. "There's a body on the floor. Aren't we going to do something about that?"

"Shhh!" they both said at once.

"Marge? Can you call Evan's room and let him know I need his assistance, please?" Alayna turned Mary toward the door. "Why don't you go find the doctor guest and see if he is willing to help us move the body."

"You want me to get Scott? It's a bit late for that, don't you think?" Mary spun around and pointed at

Jed's body. "Move it? Shouldn't you call the police? This is a crime scene! Someone murdered that man!"

Marge left the room to go call Evan while Alayna dealt with Mary's hysteria. She had no time for dramatics. "The road is snowed in. No one can get up here until at least late tomorrow. We can't leave a dead man lying here like this for that long. It's disrespectful to him, if nothing else."

Running her fingers through her hair, Mary stepped back slowly. "This is unreal. It can't be happening."

She led Mary to a chair and sat her in it. "Just stay here. I'll take care of the body."

Mary didn't respond, just sat that there murmuring to herself. Alayna left her to go and wait for Marge and Evan.

Fortunately, it didn't take long for them to return. Evan already had on his winter coat and hat. He carried hers in his hand. "I hope it's okay. Marge unlocked your door so I could grab this."

Alayna took the coat and slipped it on. "It's fine. Saves me a trip and lets us get Jed out of here more quickly."

Marge had a bedsheet with her. The worn material was covered in a faded floral print. She handed it to Alayna. "I have no idea if we have any more tarps since the barn is gone, so will this work instead?"

She accepted the sheet and shook it to open it. "This will be fine, Marge. Thank you."

"I'm going to grab my coat and slip on my boots. They're in the kitchen, so it won't take me long."

"Okay," Evan said. "We will get him wrapped up."

Marge disappeared. Mary still whimpered in her chair. Evan motioned toward her. "How did she end up in here?" He pulled his phone from his pocket. "I need to snap some photos for Chief Roman before we move him."

Alayna frowned as she glanced over at Mary. "Marge asked me to light candles. Mary followed me around demanding to know if you and I were cops. Said her brother is one and she'd recognize the tell-tale signs anywhere."

Evan walked around the body, taking pictures from different angles, until he stood by Jed's head. He bent over and studied something on the floor. "I think I found something."

"What is it?" Alayna moved over beside him to see it better.

"It looks like a note." Pulling his sleeve over his hand to avoid contaminating any evidence, he used a fabric-covered finger to slide the paper into full view.

"Oh no." Alayna took a step back, a hand over her mouth. Five words were scribbled on the sheet of paper, now stained in one corner, probably with Jed's blood.

Maybe now you're paying attention.

"We have to tell Marge." She glanced over her shoulder toward the lobby. "Or maybe we shouldn't after what happened to her this morning."

Mary got up and wandered from the room, a blank expression on her face.

"Do we need to worry about her?" Evan asked, motioning with his chin in the direction Mary had gone.

"I have no idea. But at this point, I think we need to have a talk with the other guests. This proves there is a killer in our midst, and they deserve to know."

"As much as I don't want to do this, I agree. It's time. Maybe we could get a read on who might be responsible if we pay attention." Evan set the note down and took one end of the sheet.

"Do you actually think it could be a guest?" Alayna bent and wrapped the sheet around Jed's feet while Evan covered his head. Blood immediately began to soak through the fabric, and the knife formed a little tent, but it was better than nothing.

"I don't want to think so, but honestly, I had begun to think it was Jed, and obviously I was wrong." He made a sweeping motion toward the sheet-covered body.

Alayna sighed. "I know. I had thought it was him too. Obviously, we are both rusty at crime solving."

Marge came back all decked out in her winter coat, boots, and hat. "Let's do this. And when we get back, I think it's time we tell the other guests what's been happening. I didn't want to believe it before, but one of them might be a murderer. If so, I intend to find out who."

The older woman's conviction hit Alayna straight in the heart. In less than seventy-two hours, she'd lost the three people she seemed to care about the most as well as a treasured keepsake and an entire building in a fire that could have destroyed everything she had. Alayna couldn't blame her for wanting answers. She'd be demanding them.

"We'll go out through the kitchen. It's the closest door and closest to the building where the others are." Evan squatted by Jed's head while Alayna stayed at his feet and Marge took the midsection. "You ladies ready?"

They both nodded.

"Okay, lift on three then," Evan replied. "One... two... *three!*"

As a group, they lifted Jed and carried him away. Without the high winds and blowing snow, the trek went more quickly, and they were back in the lodge in less than ten minutes.

"It's suppertime. Should we make the announcement now?" Marge asked. "Or do you want to wait until after the service is over? It won't take long to set out sandwiches and fruit."

Evan shrugged. "Let them eat first. I don't want to ruin the meal. It's not like anyone is going anywhere."

Marge went off to hang up her coat and get the kitchen staff moving, leaving Evan and Alayna alone once more.

CHAPTER FIFTEEN

ONCE DINNER HAD BEEN SERVED AND THE GUESTS HAD eaten their fill, Marge shushed everyone. She herself had cleaned up the blood on the floor in the game room and blocked both entrances with Wet Floor signs. Now she stood in the center of the dining room looking pale, fraught, and exhausted.

Marge clapped her hands together twice. "Attention, everyone! Quiet, please. We have some things we need to discuss."

The crowd kept on talking and laughing as though she wasn't there.

"Good evening, everyone! May I have your attention here, please?"

Again, they just kept on as though she weren't

there. Just as Alayna was about to get up and give them a piece of her mind, Evan stuck his fingers in his mouth and let out a loud, shrill whistle. The room fell completely silent.

"Thank you, Evan." She waved in their direction. "Now, as I tried to say before. We have some things we need to discuss."

Mary, sitting at a table near theirs, let out a little whimper. Her companion, Scott, reached over and squeezed her hand lightly. By the look on his face, Mary had told him about Jed.

There was a low rumble as people looked around and whispered questions to each other as Marge stood there, looking like she might faint again at any moment.

"I'm going to go rescue her," Alayna said to Evan, who nodded.

Alayna got up and walked to the center of the room. "I've got this, Marge, if you want to go sit with Evan."

She didn't reply but did start to walk in the direction of where Evan still sat. When she'd made it almost to the table, her legs buckled. Evan jumped up and caught her. "It's okay, Marge. Just have a seat here. I know it's been a hard day."

He got her settled, then gave Alayna a little salute. Her cue to begin.

"Hi everyone. My name is Alayna Baron. I'm a Juvenile Parole Officer for the city of Virginia Beach." She pointed at Evan, who gave a little salute to the crowd. "And that is Detective Evan Marshall of the Virginia Beach Police Department. As you know, there was an accident here a couple of days ago. One of the employees was found dead outside in the snow."

A murmur passed through the room. "It was awful," said the woman who'd first found Haley.

Alayna nodded. "Yes, I know. And I am so sorry you had to see that. But—"

"When will the police be able to get up here and take her to the morgue?" a man Alayna hadn't yet met asked.

"As soon as the roads clear. But we really need—"

"And then there was that fire this morning. I mean, what are the chances someone dies *and* a building burns down while we're all here?" This time it was a woman about five years younger than her who interrupted.

"Listen!" Alayna yelled. "The fire wasn't an accident. Haley's death probably wasn't an accident either. Or the two other deaths we've had this weekend."

"There was someone else that died?" the woman who had found Haley asked, all the color draining from her face.

"Yes. First was Frank, a male employee, and then just a short time ago we found another employee, Jed, dead. The others were made to look like accidents, but this one was obviously murder."

Mary let out a loud sob and buried her face in Scott's chest.

Everyone began to talk at once.

"Excuse me!" Alayna called over the din, but no one seemed to hear her.

Evan gave another shrill whistle, and just like the first time, the crowd fell silent at once.

She mouthed a thank-you to him, then continued her talk. "Someone destroyed the generator, so now we have no lights or electricity to get through the night. I suggest that each of you retire to your room for the evening, lock the door, and bundle up."

"Are you saying that one of us is a murderer? Is that why you want us to lock ourselves away?" Scott asked. Mary turned away from his embrace and looked at her.

"It's possible, I suppose. Although I'm thinking about keeping each of you alive more than anything. If you don't let anyone in your room, you should be safe, right?"

"What are you and the detective doing to catch the guy?" an older gentleman asked.

Alayna pushed her hair behind her ears. "Until this morning, we weren't looking for a murderer. We thought we were dealing with two accidents. Local authorities have been notified of each incident."

"What about the fire?" someone asked.

"The fire appears to be arson. Detective Marshall and I were inside when someone intentionally locked the doors, spread accelerant, and lit the building on fire."

"So, someone is after you two?" Mary asked, appearing to have calmed down considerably.

"We don't even know if they knew we were inside the barn. At this time, no one knows why these things are happening."

Marge stood up. "I am so, so sorry that this weekend hasn't been the event you signed up for. When the snowstorm hit, I didn't worry since y'all were supposed to be here for four days anyway. When my dear, sweet Haley died, I thought it was a tragic accident. But there's been too many things—I just can't keep quiet anymore. I want all of you to be safe and able to return home in one piece. When this is over, I will be processing partial refunds for everyone. Now please, do what Ms. Baron has suggested and head to your rooms for the evening."

"How do we know we will be safe there?" Scott asked, his arm wrapped around Mary.

Alayna spoke up. "Detective Marshall and I will be patrolling the lodge all night. We just need to make it through tonight and tomorrow until the police can get up here and take over."

"So, if the road is open tomorrow, we can leave?" someone called out from the back of the room.

She nodded. "If the road gets cleared out tomorrow, then yes, you should be able to leave after the police finish their interviews."

Slowly, the other guests began to disperse. Marge talked to them and assured them that everything would be just fine if they stayed in their rooms for the evening. "There are candles in every room. Please use them, and if you need matches, there is a bowl on the table by the water cooler."

There was some grumbling, but mostly people just headed up the stairs. Alayna noticed some of the guests pairing off into couples, holding hands as they walked. They'd have plenty to keep them busy that night, she'd bet.

When they were alone, Alayna sent Marge to bed.

"Are you sure you don't need me?" Marge asked.

Alayna placed her hands on Marge's arms and gently turned her toward the stairs. "You've had a really long day. Evan and I can handle this. Get some rest."

She nodded. "Thank you for everything. I have no idea what I'd have done without you here this weekend." Marge wrapped her arms around Evan and then Alayna. "The best part of all of it is I just *knew* you were meant for each other."

EVAN WATCHED THE FLUSH CREEP UP ALAYNA'S NECK as Marge gushed about her matchmaking ability. He hated to admit it, but Marge had been right as far as the type of woman he sought for a partner. He really never expected to be interested in anyone again after Christine died. Yet, here he stood, admiring the way candlelight played off the amber highlights in Alayna's hair as her fair skin turned a pretty shade of embarrassed. When she looked over at him, those big brown eyes full of so many questions, it hit him hard in the gut. They'd spent only three days together, yet he felt like they had so many more days meant to be. The attraction had been instant, and once he'd figured out who she was, he'd remembered the way he'd responded to her physically that day.

Marge hugged Alayna, then went off to her room, promising to stay there until morning.

"I haven't had this many all-nighters since college." Alayna dropped into an oversized armchair by one of the windows.

"I never went to college, but I spent many all-nighters with my brothers growing up." He sat in the chair facing her.

Alayna tilted her head to the side and studied him. "Why didn't you go to college?"

He shrugged. "I'd wanted to be a cop my whole life. Christine and I got married after high school graduation. I worked at a grocery store full-time with the plan of applying to the local police department when I turned twenty-one. Then I was a nineteen-year-old widower with no plans on how to survive, so I did what I thought was best—ran away from home."

"It breaks my heart that you have had so much

loss in your life already. It's just another thing we seem to have in common." She looked out the window into the darkness. He couldn't tell if the shadows on her face were from the candles in the room or the memories she carried.

"I can't imagine losing my parents at such a young age." He really wanted to hold her, but something held him back.

"I spent a lot of time wishing I'd died with them. And when my grandmother died too—well, there isn't anything like the loneliness you feel when you have absolutely no one left in the world."

He pulled his chair closer to hers so that he could hold her hands in his. "If there were any way for me to go back in time and change things for you, I'd do it in a heartbeat."

When she turned away from the window, he could see tears on her cheeks. His heart clenched in his chest at her obvious pain. "Maybe I'm just one of those people meant to go through life alone."

He reached for her, but she slid her chair back and out of his reach. He tried to hide his own hurt at her reaction, but he couldn't say he'd been success-ful. "You are *not* meant to be alone. Sometimes bad things happen to good people, that's all. In just a few days, I've come to care about you quite a bit. And I hope that we will have the opportunity to explore these feelings even after we go home to Virginia Beach."

Alayna jumped up and began to pace the room. "You don't understand what it's been like."

He stood up too and stopped her pacing by standing in front of her. "You're right. I have no way to understand the loss you've experienced. But I understand the heartbreak of having someone you love ripped from your life with no warning."

She reached a hand up and pressed her palm to his cheek. The sadness mixed with tenderness in her eyes nearly broke his heart. "You're a really good man, Evan Marshall. One day you will meet another woman worthy of your heart and soul. She won't replace your wife, but she will start to heal the wounds you've been carrying around for so long."

He placed his hands on the sides of her face and lifted her head, forcing her to look him in the eyes. "I think I may already have."

"We've only known each other three days. That's not nearly enough time to feel anything for anyone. You can't possibly believe in that matchmaker stuff of Marge's?"

He ran his thumb lightly along the line of her jaw, enjoying the feel of her smooth skin and the little shiver his touch seemed to elicit from her. "I didn't used to believe in it. And, honestly, it could all be crap. But I do believe in the connection I feel to you. The way you light up a room when you enter and how that lights up my soul. I believe that things happen for a reason, and the very fact that we both ended up here, in this lodge on this weekend, well, there has to be a reason."

"We've been trapped here, snowed in, with a killer for three days. Emotions are running high, adrenaline rushing through you constantly. We are convenient to each other in the situation. Those feelings will fade with the adrenaline. Once we're back at home, you'll see we have nothing in common and no actual attraction to each other."

"I think you're wrong." He leaned down and pressed his lips to hers, wrapping his arms around her and pulling her in close. How dare she say that the fireworks erupting through his entire body weren't real? How could she say that the peace he felt with her in his arms was a product of adrenaline? His feelings were young, but they were real, and based on her response to his kiss, she felt the same. No matter how hard she tried to deny it.

As he attempted to deepen the kiss, she leaned into him and wrapped her arms around his neck, instead of backing away as he'd feared. Evan delighted in the fact that he was breaking down the walls she'd erected.

She felt so perfect in his arms, like her body was designed to complement his. He slid his hands slowly down her back, letting them come to rest on her hips as he continued to lose himself in the most amazing kiss of his life.

They backed up until her legs touched the sofa. He spun them around so that he dropped on to the cushion, pulling her into his lap, never once breaking their connection.

Tangling his hands in her hair, he marveled at the softness of her waves. "Alayna," he murmured against her lips. "I can't tell you how happy it makes me that we both ended up here together."

She pulled back a tiny bit, resting her forehead against his and pressing her palm lightly against his cheek. "I'm feeling pretty happy about it myself."

He couldn't stop the grin that spread over his lips. "Good." He kissed her again, soft and gentle. "If we make it out of here alive, I'm taking you on a real date back home in Virginia Beach."

"Let's not get ahead of ourselves." She laughed. "I'm just hoping to make it out of here alive. The rest will figure itself out. Maybe."

Maybe? What the heck was that supposed to mean? Before he could ask, she climbed off of his lap and moved out of his reach.

"I'm going to check the upstairs floors. Why don't you do a double check on the windows and doors down here?"

Without waiting for his reply, she walked away.

Still a little high from their kiss, he made a slow loop of the main floor, checking doors and windows for what felt like the tenth time that day. Alayna had kissed him like she really meant it, then had said *maybe* they'd see each other when they got home. Why was she so afraid of him? Had he been stupid to let himself think maybe he could have love again? Maybe Christine really had been his one and only. He should be grateful he'd had that. Some people never even knew a love like that once in their life.

In the game room, he stopped in the place where they'd found Jed. The note the killer left behind still sat on a table. Pulling his sleeve over his hand again and grabbing it only by one corner, he carried it to the kitchen and found a paper bag to put it in. The blood that had soaked one edge had long since dried, but he still didn't want to risk contaminating any possible DNA evidence.

He took the bag out to the lobby to wait for

Alayna to return, but she never did. He could hear her moving around in the kitchen at one point, but she didn't join him in the lobby. Her absence left him feeling lonely and a little empty. Memories of his life with Christine played through his mind like a movie reel. As he sat there, alone in the candlelight, he replayed every moment of their relationship, from their first date to the day she died in his arms. When he reached that last heartbreaking memory, he had a good, solid cry, then took the whole story and tucked it away in the back of his mind. He'd mourned his wife and baby for a decade. It was time to move forward. And he wanted to move forward with Parole Office Alayna Baron.

Now if he could just convince her to give it a go.

As he sat in the chair watching the horizon lighten, Alayna appeared dressed in her winter gear. "I'm going to take a walk and see if I can figure out what happened to our squatter. I'll lock the door on my way out. I can't help but think he might be the key to all of this."

She made no mention of their talk—or kiss—the night before. Alayna was all business. He wanted to force her to face their feelings together, but he also knew her just well enough to know that this was not the time for that. So, he'd go along with her little *nothing to see here* plan and save the big talk for after this was over. Maybe during the long ride back to Virginia Beach. She'd have nowhere to run then.

Smiling at the thought, he stood up. "Great idea. Let me get my coat and I'll go with you."

CHAPTER SIXTEEN

HE MET ALAYNA AT THE FRONT DOOR WITH A SMILE. He'd decided to shelve the other discussion until later. "Let's do this."

Without replying, she opened the door and stepped out onto the porch. A brisk chill met them, making him shiver.

"I really need to get back to the beach." Alayna hugged herself. "This cold is getting ridiculous."

He almost put an arm around her shoulders but changed his mind at the last minute. They needed to have a certain conversation first. Instead, he just moved a little faster. The snow had become hard packed, which made it easier for him to move around with the boot on.

"How's your foot doing?" Alayna asked. "You've really pushed yourself this weekend."

Evan shrugged. "It's okay. I've kind of gotten used to the low-grade ache. My doctor is probably going to have a fit though when he sees this thing." He pointed as his boot. The hard plastic had gotten pretty nasty, between the snow and the fire and everything else.

They passed the locked building with all the bodies in it and continued on to a large shed. "Look." Alayna stopped walking and looked down. "Footprints."

The tracks looked similar to the ones they'd seen by the barn. Evan followed them with his eyes. "They appear to go past this shed and down to that other small barn over there."

Halfway down a low grade, nestled between the hill they stood on and the side of a tree-covered mountain, sat a building that looked like a miniature of the burned barn. Alayna began the trek toward it, taking a wide arc away from the tracks. She waved him on to join her. "If we take it wide and stay along the tree line, maybe it's still dim enough out here he won't see us coming."

"Sounds like a plan."

They worked their way through the snow-covered field slowly, keeping an eye on the barn and surrounding area for any squatters.

"Do you have your gun?" Evan asked as they got close.

"Always."

He turned to look over his shoulder. She already had her weapon out and ready. "If you ever want to change departments, we could use another good detective."

"Thanks. I like my job. Although I do think we make a good team."

Fortunately, he was in front of Alayna and she couldn't see him grinning like a fool. "I'd definitely have to agree with that assessment."

They reached the side of the barn. Evan pressed a finger to his lips then took two steps forward, crouching beneath a small window. Slowly he moved up until he reached eye level with the sill. Peering inside, there was only darkness. Dropping back down below the window, he moved back to where Alayna waited. "It's too dark inside to see much."

She frowned, pressing two fingers to her temple. "Assuming a similar floor plan, there might be a back entrance like on the big barn. We could maybe sneak in that way."

"Good idea." He moved alongside the weathered building until he reached the corner. With his gun in position in front of him, he slowly turned the corner. "It's clear."

Alayna stepped up behind him. "There's the door."

He nodded and they moved together, guns prone and ready. At this point, he had no idea what to expect anymore. When they reached the door, he stepped to the other side and grabbed the handle. Alayna gave a nod, and he yanked the door open. They both moved back, half expecting a rain of gunfire. Everything stayed silent though, so after a bit, Evan stepped inside. Alayna entered as well, to his right. He scanned the space but saw nothing. Just like in the larger barn, there were three doors along one wall leading to various rooms. A few boxes and miscellaneous lawn implements had been stacked against one wall. The smell of old hay and mildew filled the room.

"There's disturbances in the dust and dirt on the floor," Alayna whispered. "See? It looks like something has been dragged to that office over there."

"Hmm… could have been a cot and a duffle bag," Evan whispered back as he moved forward, watching the marks on the ground as he walked. His breath came out in little cloudy puffs as the chill of the building wrapped around him. The marks led straight to the door that matched the one in the larger barn. He looked over at Alayna. "You ready?"

She nodded, and they repeated the same process as they did at the back door to the structure.

As the office door slammed open, he waited a second time for someone or something to react, but nothing happened. They stepped into the room as Alayna shined her light around the space.

"Do you always have the flashlight with you?" Evan asked as he inspected the room.

"Since I was a kid. I hated the dark. Now it's as much a habit as putting on my shoes." She stopped moving the light as it focused on a cot in a corner. "I think our squatter found a new home."

"Or our killer." Evan crossed the room to the makeshift bed. A blanket had been tossed haphazardly on the pillow. Under the bed he found a bag with the zipper left open. He pulled the bag out and peered inside. Right on top of the clothes was a stack of papers. Using the light on his cell phone to scan the papers, he couldn't believe what he saw. At the top, the name of a local attorney's office was printed. Below the heading he saw the words *Blue Ridge Lodge* and Marge's name.

"Alayna?" He waved her over. "Come look at this."

"What did you find?" She walked over and squatted beside him. "That looks like a sales contract."

Evan scanned the rest of the page. "It is. It's a proposal to purchase the lodge. Did Marge say anything to you about selling?"

She shook her head. "Only that her ex wanted to claim his half."

He flipped the pages and stopped on the second-to-last one. "Isn't her ex's name Henry?"

"Yes," Alayna said.

"I think we figured out who the squatter is." Evan folded the papers up and tucked them in the inside pocket of his jacket.

"And maybe our killer too." Alayna ran her flashlight around the room once more. "We need to go tell Marge."

"I really hope they get that road cleared out today." He stood up. "It's still early. Maybe we can talk to Marge before the other guests come down to have breakfast."

Evan closed the office door and the barn door as they left. The walk back to the lodge passed quickly.

"Do you think it's Henry committing the murders?" Alayna asked.

"I couldn't say for sure."

"And locking us in the barn? Setting it on fire?" Her building stress was obvious.

He reached over and clasped her hand. "I believe an uninvited guest has been living on the property, but we don't know for sure who it is. Or why. It could be Henry, or maybe he hired someone."

Alayna pulled her hand from his and shoved it in her pocket. "Like a hit man?"

He shrugged, ignoring the pang of sadness that hit him when she pulled away. "I wish I knew. Right now, I just know that Marge should see these papers. I think it's her ex that has been living here."

They climbed the front porch steps, and Evan unlocked the front door with a key he'd found in the kitchen on one of his rounds the night before. Remembering he hadn't slept in way too long, he let out a big yawn. "I'm going to sleep for a week when I get home."

Alayna laughed. "Yeah, I'm pretty much running on adrenaline and stubbornness at this point."

They stepped inside, and Evan locked the door behind them. "I think I hear someone in the kitchen. Maybe it's Marge."

Alayna pointed to a chandelier in the center of the lobby. "The lights are back on."

Evan pulled his jacket off as they walked and slung it over his arm. "That's a good sign. It means the road is getting cleared."

"Good." Alayna took her jacket off as well and set it behind the reception desk. She held out her hand for his. "Want me to put yours back here too?"

"Thanks." He handed her the jacket. "Are you anxious to get out of here?" He didn't really want to know. Leaving might mean he and Alayna would go their separate ways, and that didn't sit well with him.

"I don't know." She shrugged. "Maybe. I really just want to put an end to whatever has been happening here."

"Do you smell that?" He breathed deeply and rubbed his abdomen. "Bacon."

Alayna laughed. "Do all the men in your family love food the way you do?"

"Come on, it's *bacon*. Who doesn't love meat candy?"

"*Meat candy*? Evan Marshall, you are something else!"

"Oh, there you are!" Marge appeared from the kitchen. "Bacon, eggs, and waffles for breakfast today. The power came back on!"

"Marge? We need to talk to you about something." Alayna led her to a chair. "It's probably better if you sit down."

"Did something else happen?" Marge sat down with her hands clasped tightly in her lap.

Evan handed her the papers they'd found. "Have you ever seen these before?"

They both watched as Marge scanned the pages. "Yes. My ex-husband brought them here a couple of weeks ago. I sent him away. I am *not* selling him my property." She handed them back to Evan. "I don't— where did *you* find them?"

"There's a little barn at the back of the property." Evan motioned in the direction of the barn.

Marge nodded. "Yes. Daddy used to keep our personal horses down there in the warmer months."

"We found them there. In one of the offices."

She looked confused. "I don't understand."

Alayna perched on the arm of the chair and wrapped an arm around Marge's shoulders. "Someone has been living in there. We found a cot and a duffle bag. The papers were in the bag."

Marge looked at Alayna, then over at him. "Henry has been the one squatting on my property. But why?"

Evan picked up her hand and held it between both of his. "Marge, we think maybe he's the one responsible for... all the things that have been happening this weekend."

Marge jumped to her feet, her hands to her chest. "I told you he was a bad man. Did he set the barn on fire too?"

"It's possible," Evan replied.

"But he knew they were like family to me!" Tears fell from her eyes. "How could he? How could he?" She stopped and turned to look at them. "Why did he have those papers? He knew I'd never sell to him. Not without a massive fight."

Evan shrugged. "I'm just not sure, Marge. Maybe he just hoped he could scare you into it? There must be tremendous potential with the lodge."

"I make a really good living. Daddy worked hard to give us a top dollar name in the resort world." She pressed her fingertips to her temples. "I'm not feeling so wonderful." Marge collapsed for the second time in as many days.

ALAYNA FELT COMPLETELY HELPLESS. WHEN MARGE fainted, Evan managed to catch her and set her back in the chair. Alayna jumped up to get a glass of cold water. While she filled the glass, a loud scream sounded in the lobby. Alayna dropped the glass into the sink and sprinted back to the lobby.

Marge knelt on the ground next to Evan, who lay on the hardwood, a trail of blood running down the side of this temple.

"What happened?" She dropped to her knees. "Marge! What happened?"

"I don't know! One minute he was teasing me about wanting to faint in his arms, and the next he said 'ouch,' stumbled backward, tripped, and smacked his head on the side table."

Alayna jumped up and ran over to the windows. Smack in the center of one of them was a tiny hole. Someone had fired a small caliber weapon at the glass. Movement at the wood line caught her eye. Pressing her face to the glass, she could just make out a figure weaving in and out of the trees. She ran back to Evan. "Is he bleeding anywhere else?"

"I don't think so!" Marge ran her hands frantically over Evan's chest. "I don't see anything."

Alayna ran to the door. "Stay here, Marge. No matter what happens, don't let anyone outside!"

She pulled open the door and ran outside. Yanking her gun from the holster on her hip, Alayna ran as fast she could, trying to get to the back of the building. The sun had fully risen and begun to melt the snow. Running in slush was much harder than the crunchy snow they'd trudged through that morning.

At the end of the building, she stopped and listened. Hearing nothing, she looked around the corner, making sure it was clear before racing to the other edge. As she reached the back corner, she stopped again, listened, and then peeked around the wall. A shot flew past her head so close, she nearly felt a breeze.

Alayna ducked back behind the cover of the building. "Henry! It's over! Drop your gun!"

"You got something that's mine, and I want it back!" he yelled, his voice shrill.

Two more bullets flew by, so close she heard the whistle as they passed. "Why are you trying to kill me? I don't even know you!"

The only reply was another gunshot.

"Haven't you killed enough people? That poor girl, she didn't deserve what you did to her! And what about Frank? And Jed! They didn't do anything to you!"

Two more shots rang out.

She jumped out and fired two shots of her own, then ducked back around the corner of the lodge.

"Stand down, Henry! This isn't how to get what you want!"

"It ain't me shootin'! I just want my paperwork back! I know the two of ya took them outta my bag this morning!"

His voice sounded a lot closer than it had. He'd been moving in on her—distracting her with conversation so he could make his move. She had to do something. Alayna stuck her gun around the edge of the building and pulled the trigger, hoping to make contact with her bullet.

Henry cursed. "Stop shooting at me! I *told you* it ain't me shootin' at you!"

From around the other side of the house, she heard Evan call out. "Alayna! Where are you? *Alayna*!"

"Oh, goodie! Your boyfriend is coming to your rescue!" Henry taunted her, sounding even closer than moments before. "Is he the one tryna kill me?"

"He's not my boyfriend. We hardly know each other! And stop lying! I know it's you trying to shoot me!"

"I am *not*!" Henry laughed, nastiness dampening all the humor. "Do you always kiss people you don't know?"

"*Alayna*!" Evan had pure panic in his voice.

Alayna backed up along the side of the building, back toward Evan's voice and the front of the lodge. "How many more people are you going to kill?" she called to Henry. "You're already going to go to prison for a very long time."

Alayna heard two more shots. Henry howled in pain. Another shot fired, echoing over the snow-covered ground.

"Alayna! Are you okay?" Evan stumbled toward her, looking unsteady as he half jogged, half dragged himself through the snow.

"There's someone else shooting, Evan. Henry's down!"

Evan reached for his gun as he neared her. "Alayna! Get out of the way!"

The expression on his face unnerved Alayna as he ran at her, gun pointed straight at her chest. His eyes though, they looked right through her as though she weren't even there. "*Move, Alayna!*"

Alayna spun and came face-to-face with Marge and her twenty-two-caliber rifle. Her eyes held a wild look that matched the craziness of her wind-blown hair.

"This old lodge and a stupid stuffed bear aren't the only thing my daddy left me." She motioned with the barrel of the rifle. "Get over there by hero boy."

"What are you doing, Marge?" Evan inched closer, his gun aimed straight at the older woman. "Drop your gun! This ends now!"

"You're damn right it does! If the two of you had minded your own business, it would have been him in that barn! Everyone would have blamed him for the murders, and I would have gotten my revenge!"

"You're not making any sense, Marge!" Alayna, holding her hands in the air in front of her, took a couple of steps back. From the corner of her eye, she caught sight of several of the guests huddled at the corner of the lodge.

"She did it, Alayna. Haley, Frank, Jed, the barn. Even the bear, right, Marge?" Evan took two more steps toward Marge.

"Stop!" Marge yelled. "Don't come any closer! The two of you ruined everything! They would have blamed Henry for all of it! Just like I planned. He'd have gone to prison and left my home alone." She waved the rifle wildly in the air. A strong gust of icy wind blew past them, causing Marge to stumble forward.

As she caught herself, a loud blast filled the air. Evan collapsed, his gun falling from his hand and sliding along the hard crust of the snow. The moment his body hit the ground, snow around him began to stain red.

"*No*! Evan!" Alayna charged at Marge, plowing into the other woman and slamming her to the ground. "I need some help! Call 911! Hang on, Evan! Don't leave me! I'll be right there!"

Riding high on the adrenaline coursing through her veins, Alayna flipped Marge onto her stomach and held her wrists behind her back.

"It's my property! Henry tried to take it away from me!" Marge kicked her feet, bucking her hips. "Let me go!"

Alayna pinned Marge to the ground with her knee. "So you killed the people that loved you? Sure doesn't make sense to me." Finally noticing the crowd that had gathered, she called out, "Mary!"

"I had to do something!" Marge growled.

The young couple ran over, looking totally freaked out. Mary rubbed her hands up and down her arms. "Oh my God, Alayna! Are you okay?"

Scott dropped into the snow next to Evan. "I'm a doctor."

He gently rolled Evan over. Alayna sucked in a breath at all the blood on the snow. "He's hit in the belly, isn't he?"

Scott pulled at Evan's clothes. "Yes, and it looks bad."

Evan gasped for breath and moaned in pain.

"I should have aimed higher!" Marge shouted, from her position facedown in the snow. "He ruined everything!"

"Shut up!" Alayna tightened her hold on Marge's wrists.

"Hold on, man." Scott put pressure on the wound. "He's lost a lot of blood. Did someone call 911 yet?" he yelled to the crowd.

"I did!" one of the guests yelled back. "The road is clear! Help is on the way!"

"Mary!" Alayna called. "I need you to get me something to bind her wrists with. Can you do that?"

Mary nodded frantically and took off toward the lodge.

"How is he?" Alayna yelled to Scott. Evan's face had lost so much color, he nearly matched the snow. Her heart was torn between going to him and keeping Marge contained.

"Still holding on, but he's getting weaker."

"Where is that ambulance?" Her heart pounding in her chest, Alayna fought back the urge to pick Evan up, run to his Jeep, and drive him to the hospital herself. With the adrenaline still coursing full force through her body, she could probably run all the way down the mountain.

Mary returned quickly. She leaned down and handed something shiny to Alayna. She grabbed them and snapped them around Marge's wrists. "Where did you find handcuffs?"

The other woman turned a bright crimson color. "In my suitcase."

"Are you a cop too?" Alayna asked, dragging Marge to her feet.

Mary flushed an even deeper red. "Um, no."

Despite what was happening around her, Alayna let out a little laugh. "Well, I'm glad you had them with you." Tugging Marge's arm, she dragged her over to where Evan lay in the snow, Scott holding pressure on his wound. "You better hope he lives."

Overhead, the loud chop-chop sound of a helicopter filled the air.

"Look!" Mary pointed up. "They brought in the chopper!"

"Where they gonna land that bird?" one of the guests asked.

Before anyone could answer, the pilot passed over them and landed perfectly in a clearing a few hundred feet away. Several medical personnel jumped out and ran toward them carrying a back board.

"What happened here?" one of them asked, immediately arranging the board to load Evan on.

"Gunshot wound to the abdomen," Scott said. "I'm a doctor. I've been holding pressure as best I can. He lost a lot of blood, but I think the cold air is helping slow the flow."

"Thank you, Doctor. We'll take it from here."

One of the doctors ran over to Henry and felt for a pulse. He shook his head. "This one's gone!" He ran back to where the others worked on Evan.

In less than a minute, they had him strapped on to the board and were running back to the helicopter. Alayna had absolutely no chance to beg Evan not to die on her.

As the helicopter lifted off, Alayna watched it disappear over the tops of the trees with tears running down her face. She swiped at the wetness with her free hand as she led Marge to the front porch. Sirens sounded in the distance. Pretty soon the police would be there and take over. Then she could concentrate on finding a way to get to the hospital to be with Evan.

"Why are you wasting your tears on *him*?" Marge sneered. "That boy is damaged. Even more than you."

"What about your matchmaking gift, Marge? Was that a lie too?" Alayna didn't really care what the woman had to say. She'd had way more than enough of Marge, the Blue Ridge Lodge, and anything having to do with either.

Several police cars came racing into the parking lot, sirens screaming and tires spinning. Officers jumped from the cars, guns in hand and running toward them.

"It's okay!" Alayna yelled to them. "The threat has been neutralized! She's here, cuffed and ready to go!"

Two officers bounded up the stone steps followed by an older man whose name tag read Roman.

"I'm Chief Roman. Where's Detective Marshall?"

"I shot him." Marge grinned a wild, frightening grin.

The chief turned to Alayna, his expression full of questions. She shook her head. "That helicopter that just left? Evan's in it. Belly wound from a twenty-two-caliber rifle."

CHAPTER SEVENTEEN

"OH, MAN." THE CHIEF SHOOK HIS HEAD. "IS HE GOING to make it?" He waved to some of the officers, and one of them headed their way.

Alayna shrugged. "There was a whole lotta blood."

"I'll take her in." The uniformed officer took Marge by the arm and led her away.

Chief Roman looked at the remains of the barn and then over to the body of Marge's ex-husband, now covered with a blanket. "Been one heck of a weekend, hasn't it?"

"She killed them all, Chief. Including Henry. And maybe Evan." The last name came out with a little sob.

Alayna suddenly felt weak. She walked over to

the porch steps and lowered herself slowly to the cold stone. She still didn't have a jacket on, but the cold seemed to have no effect on her already numb body.

"You okay, miss? You're starting to worry me." The chief waved over another officer. "Call a second medic, would ya?"

"Yes, sir." The officer nodded and stepped away, speaking into his radio.

Chief Roman leaned on the handrail with his thumbs hooked on his duty belt. "So, tell me what happened."

Alayna sagged with exhaustion. Someone dropped a wool blanket on her shoulders, which she pulled in tight. "Where should I start?"

"I'd say the best place would be the beginning."

"Well, the day we got here, someone vandalized Marge's giant stuffed bear. Hacked its head off with a machete and poured red liquid on the neck to look like blood. Then, of course, you already know about Haley."

Chief Roman nodded. "Damn shame too. I notified her parents, and they are in denial."

Alayna shivered, hugging the blanket to herself. "I can't even imagine what they are feeling. I'm so sorry for them, especially now that it looks like it was murder and not an accident."

"Oh?" The chief looked at her with a dozen questions in his gray eyes.

"Marge's ex-husband Henry had been squatting in the barn." She motioned to the pile of rubble. "But when we discovered someone had been living in there, he didn't like it. We thought he locked us in and lit the place on fire."

"He tried to burn you alive?" The disbelief on the chief's face was obvious.

"Not him. Marge. We managed to break out through one of the walls, literally in the nick of time."

"You know it was her?" Chief Roman asked.

Alayna nodded. "She admitted to it. And to killing Frank and Jed as well."

"Right. Evan called me after each death."

She sighed. "That one was the worst. We found Jed with a knife still in him. He's in the same shed with Frank and Haley. The knife the killer used is still in the body. I'd guess you'll find Marge's prints on it."

"Detective Marshall also mentioned a note."

"Yes." Alayna stood up, still holding her blanket wrapped around her. "And I know Evan took pictures of all the scenes. I just don't know where his phone is. And Marge cleaned up the blood from Jed's murder before we had a chance to do anything with that—but there are photos of the body."

Chief Roman nodded and kicked at a clump of snow. "This is gonna be one heck of a mess."

"I never should have left Virginia Beach." She laughed, without humor. "This sure wasn't the weekend my roommate promised me."

Mary appeared on the porch with a mug and handed it to Alayna. "I thought you might need something warm."

"Thank you." The cup held steaming brown liquid. Coffee. "How's everyone else?"

The other woman shrugged. "As well as can be expected I guess. Most of them are packing to leave, or talking about it anyway. Are you going to the hospital?"

Alayna looked at Chief Roman. "As soon as he says I can."

A long black hearse pulled into the drive and parked in front of the lodge. A very tall, very thin man with a full silver beard stepped out of the car. "Mornin', Chief."

The chief nodded at the older man. "Good morning, Jack. My boys are 'round back, processing the body and the scene. Soon as they give you the go-ahead, you can remove it."

"Thank you kindly." Jack strode to the back of his car and pulled open the door. He pulled out a gurney, laid a black body bag on it, and recruited one of the officers milling around to help him carry it to where Henry's body was.

"I'd like to go to the hospital now," Alayna said. "If you don't need me anymore?"

"I'll get one of my men to take you after you change and clean up."

Alayna looked down at her clothes, seeing blood smeared all over her sweater and jeans. Evan's blood. A ball of emotion formed in her throat that threatened to cut off her air supply. The dizziness set in fast as her vision blurred. "I—I don't feel so great."

The hot coffee splashed over the side of the mug, burning her hand. Alayna dropped the cup in the snow as she grabbed for the stair rail.

"Are you okay?" Chief Roman grasped her elbow and supported her to a seated position on the steps again.

"The adrenaline is wearing off, I guess. I really want to go see about Evan."

"No one will tell you anything," Scott said from a few a feet away. "You're not family."

She looked up at the man who had tried to help Evan. "I should call his mother. Evan said she lives near here. I think one or two of his brothers are cops around here too. If something happens... they need to know." Her voice broke on a little sob.

Chief Roman wrapped an arm around Alayna's shoulder. "How about I send you off to the hospital now and you can give a statement to my officer at the hospital. How does that sound?"

"She won't get any real information. She's not family," Scott said again.

"Yes," the chief agreed. "But as long as she's okay with that, then I think it would be good for her to be nearby when he gets out of surgery. Be there to meet his mother and tell her what happened."

Alayna nodded. "I want to go."

Chief Roman motioned to an officer that stood near a parked car. "You go with Officer Jansen, and I'll put in some calls to the area police departments to see if I can reach Marshall's family."

She grasped his hand. "You'd do that?"

He gave her a gentle smile. "Of course I would. We take care of our own."

It could have been the adrenaline dump or the roller coaster of emotions she'd experienced over the last four days, but she couldn't stop herself from wrapping her arms around the older man in a big hug. "Thank you so much, Chief."

The ride to the hospital felt like it took hours. Alayna, completely exhausted, went in and out of sleep, dozing and then remembering where she was and why and jerking awake again. When they reached the hospital, Officer Jansen led the way into the emergency room.

"Hey, Meredith." He gave the lady at the check-in desk a brilliant smile. "I just had a shooting victim brought in, an Evan Marshall. Belly wound."

Meredith twirled a piece of hair on her finger as she smiled back at the police officer. Alayna fought back the urge to smack them both.

"Is he alive?" Alayna demanded, her hands gripping the edge of the counter.

Meredith glanced over at her and narrowed her eyes at the bloodstains on Alayna's clothes. "Are you injured?"

"No! It's not my blood—" Officer Jansen placed a hand on her shoulder, stopping her midsentence.

"Where is the victim?" he asked Meredith.

"They took him straight to the OR." Meredith gave a sideways glance to Alayna. "That's all I can say right now."

Officer Jansen gave her another brilliant smile,

making Meredith blush. "Thank you, Meredith. You're amazing as always."

Gripping her elbow lightly, he led Alayna away from the desk, down a couple of hallways, and into a large, mostly empty waiting area.

"I need to know if Evan is okay." Alayna stopped walking in the center of the room.

"I'm sorry, but this is as close as you will be able to get until his family arrives." He motioned to a couple of chairs in the far corner. "How about we sit and talk about what has been happening at the lodge and the shooting today?"

She nodded, barely comprehending the words he said.

It took almost an hour for her to relay all that had happened at the lodge. In between pacing and studying the large screen with surgery patients' statuses on it every five minutes, she eventually got it all out. As she finished describing Marge shooting Evan, tears ran down her cheeks.

Officer Jansen patted her arm. "I'm so sorry for all you've been through. If there is anything I, or the department, can do, please don't hesitate to call." He jotted down a couple of numbers on a notecard he pulled from his pocket and handed it to her. "I really hope he pulls through."

"Thanks," she murmured, putting the paper in her pocket. "Me too."

Once she was alone, Alayna let the tears fall unchecked. Not since her parents' death had her heart hurt so badly. Not even the day Justin abandoned her felt the way Evan being shot in front of her did.

If he didn't make it….

If he died, she'd never get the chance to tell him how she felt.

How *did* she feel?

The way her heart ached, it was entirely possible she was falling in love with Evan Marshall.

"OH, GOOD. YOU'RE FINALLY AWAKE." A NURSE entered the dimly lit room. "How are you feeling?"

He grunted. His head felt way too heavy, and his tongue practically stuck to the roof of his mouth. He coughed a little, but his voice still came out really raspy. "Like someone shot me in the gut. How long have I been out?"

The nurse laughed. "About four days. My name is Isabelle. I'll be taking care of you tonight. I've been here with you all week. Where did your young lady get off to?"

"What are you talking about?" Evan tried to shift in the bed, but the pain stopped him in his tracks. He groaned.

Isabelle stepped up to check his pulse. "About my height, long wavy hair, and big brown eyes."

"Alayna was here?"

"Yes, sir. I could barely get her to step out to eat or get a little sleep." Isabelle held a temperature reader up to his temple. "She's been taking turns with your mama, watching over you."

Evan turned his head to look at Isabelle as she made some notes in his electronic chart. "My mother has been here?"

Isabelle nodded. "She's been here since the night you came in. The two of them and a couple of real handsome law enforcement types too." She made a little whistling sound. "A couple of total hotties."

Someone had called his mom and his brothers.

"I only just met Alayna a few days ago. We've been through a lot together though. Getting stranded at the lodge. The fire. The murders—"

"Oh my gosh! You were staying at the Blue Ridge Lodge? Is that how this happened?"

"Yeah." He leaned his head back and closed his eyes. "You've heard?"

"It's been all over the papers and news how that woman just snapped and started killing people. Blamed her ex-husband for it all, but he's dead too. Turns out she shot him too."

Thank goodness it wasn't Alayna's shots that killed him. She'd have a hard time with that.

"Can I have something to drink?" His tongue felt glued to the roof of his mouth.

She poured some water from a little pink container into a plastic cup and handed it to him. "Start slow, sweetie. It's been a while, you don't want to shock your system. Vomiting is gonna hurt."

He held the cup to his lips and took a tiny sip. Water had never tasted so perfect. Isabelle's warning forgotten, he took a long swallow. The second the cool liquid hit his stomach, waves of nausea kicked up, eliciting a low moan.

"Too much too fast?" She handed him a little puke bowl, but he waved it away.

"I'm fine," he grunted.

"Not as fine as those two cowboys you had visiting you." Isabelle pursed her lips and made a kissing sound.

"Gee thanks. You always kick a man when he's

down? I never could compete with any of my brothers."

She laughed. "It's not that at all. I just know when a man is off the market, and you, sweetie, are a taken man."

"I am not!" He closed his eyes against a wave of nausea, not even sure why he felt the need to argue. "Ugh."

"I'll be back in two hours. Just press that button on the rail if you need me before then." Isabelle walked to the curtain and pushed it open. Before leaving, she turned back to Evan. "Tell her how you feel. She loves you."

Isabelle sounded completely confident in her assessment. She didn't know Alayna like he did. Not that he really knew her, did he?

As he drifted back to sleep, the last time he'd seen Alayna, holding her gun on Henry, filled his mind. Along with the fear that he might lose her. This time the fear came from a completely different place—his heart.

CHAPTER EIGHTEEN

Recovery was slow. He spent too many days in the hospital, and by the time the doctor said he could go home, over a week had passed.

"You look amazing." Isabelle, his favorite nurse, entered the private room they'd finally moved him to. "I heard you were being discharged, so I had to sneak down and say goodbye."

Evan grunted as he tried to stand up. "I don't feel so amazing."

"What I meant was, you have normal color in your face again, and it looks amazing." Isabelle offered him a hand and helped him stand. Between the wound to his abdomen and his bum foot, he might never get back to work.

"I'll take your word on it."

"I'm so glad that you get to go home, but I'll miss you and your sassy personality. When's your lady coming to get you?"

"Actually, my mother is coming I think. Or one of my brothers. Whoever has my Jeep, I guess."

Isabelle frowned. "You're not planning on driving, are you?"

"Well, yeah, eventually. I live in Virginia Beach. I have to get back there somehow." Evan lowered himself into the vinyl chair in the corner of the room. "Ah, that feels much better than the bed."

She looked worried. "I'm pretty sure the doctor is going to tell you no driving for a while."

He gave Isabelle his best smile. "Don't worry about me. I'll be good. I have five brothers. Someone will make sure I get home, I promise. Thank you for taking such good care of me when I was in ICU."

She reached down and squeezed his hand lightly. "You're so welcome. Take care of yourself. Don't take this the wrong way, but I hope I never see you again."

Isabelle left the room, leaving him alone with his thoughts.

The first thing he'd do when he got back home was find Alayna and tell her exactly how he felt about her.

He'd fallen in love with Alayna Baron, and he

wanted her and the entire world to know it. Her first though, of course. Evan laughed, the sound filling the room and his heart. It had been a really long time since he'd experienced the joy and peace of loving someone.

A knock on the door interrupted his thoughts. "Come in."

The door opened, and Alayna appeared. His heart immediately skipped into high gear. Evan pushed himself to his feet, one hand holding his abdomen and the other gripping the arm of the chair.

"Alayna." He swallowed against the rise of emotion trying to escape. "I was expecting my mother or one of my brothers. I'm getting out of here today. I thought you'd gone back home. Not that I'm not happy to see you. I am."

He forced himself to stop rambling.

She looked as nervous as he felt, twisting her winter hat in her hands. "I called your mom and told her I'd come instead."

He took a step closer to her. "She was okay with that?"

Alayna smiled. "As long as I promised to bring you to her house for dinner and a good night's rest in a real bed."

"That sounds like my mom." He laughed, kind of.

It came out more like a nervous grunt. "So, you met my family, I hear."

"Isabelle?" she asked.

He grinned. "Yeah. She's great, isn't she?"

Alayna nodded. "Yeah. Really great."

"I really thought you went back to Virginia Beach." He took another step toward Alayna.

She shook her head. "I couldn't leave, not until I knew you'd be okay."

"You haven't visited since—since I woke up." One last step put him close enough to wrap her in his arms, but he refrained, no matter how much the sweet scent of her beckoned him to.

"Oh, Evan! I thought she killed you! And then you wouldn't wake up after the surgery and...." Tears poured down her cheeks as she stood there. He reached for her, but she held up a hand, telling him no. "I think I've fallen in love you, Evan. I don't know how or why, since we've really only just met. But the thought of losing you...."

Her words wrapped around his heart, sending warmth through his entire body. He raised his hands in front of him. "As you can see, I'm fine. Or I will be in a few weeks."

She clapped her hand over her mouth as another

sob took over. "I'm so sorry, Evan. I shouldn't be putting all of this on you. Not now."

He reached for her, but Alayna took a step back. He frowned. "Why are you so convinced that you aren't enough?"

She narrowed his eyes at him, wiping away her tears with her hat. "Come on, Evan. You know what happened to me."

"That man was an idiot. His actions had nothing to do with you. He was a fool to let you go. You're smart, live life with a passion that is hard to emulate, and you're absolutely beautiful. *He* didn't deserve *you*. Do you understand me? None of it was about you."

Tears filled her eyes, overflowing onto her cheeks. Evan reached up and wiped the salty water away with his fingertips. "I'm so damaged, Evan."

"So am I. But it's okay."

She looked up at him. "What do you mean?"

Evan picked up both of her hands and pressed a kiss to the back of each one. "I'm pretty sure I'm falling in love with you too, and I know I am not going anywhere. Hopefully ever. At the very least, we have a connection that I think is worth pursuing."

"How can either one of us be falling in love when we hardly know each other?"

He laughed. "I'm decisive. When I know what I want, I go for it. And what I want right now is the chance to prove to you that you are worthy of love. *My* love. I'm a patient man. I'll wait until you see what I already know." He stepped in close and wrapped her in a gentle embrace, ignoring the ache in his abdomen in lieu of the one in his heart that needed tending.

The moment their lips touched, he knew for sure —Alayna was the woman for him. This kiss felt different than the other times he been lucky enough to kiss her. Emotions he'd missed wrapped around him as he kissed her with his heart as much as his lips.

She nodded against him. "Okay."

He pulled back a little and looked deep into her eyes. "Okay, like stop kissing you, or okay, you're willing to give us a chance?"

She reached over and grasped the front of his sweater, pulling him back to her. "Well, don't stop kissing me."

"Your wish is my command."

As Evan pressed his lips to hers once more, he knew his life would never be the same. Second chances only came along once, and he had no intention of letting go without a fight.

THANKS FOR READING *MURDER ON THE MOUNTAIN*. I do hope you enjoyed Evan and Alayna's story. If you haven't done so already, be sure to check out Adam's story, Murder on the Mountain.

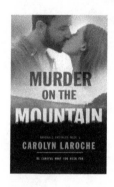

I appreciate your help in spreading the word, including telling a friend. Before you go, it would mean so much to me if you would take a few minutes to write a review and share how you feel about my story so others may find my work. Reviews really do help readers find books. Please leave a review on your favorite book site.

Be sure to also join my newsletter to receive all the news first: Join my newsletter: www.carolyn-laroche.wordpress.com

ACKNOWLEDGMENTS

The world's biggest thank you goes to Becky Johnson for hearing me out *and* considering my idea for this book. Another huge thank you to Olivia Ventura, the most amazing editor for not only taking on this particular project under its unique time constraints but for fully understanding my brain and my where I want books to go.

Her suggestions made this story beyond amazing. Thank you to the proofreader, beta readers, and everyone else who has had a hand in this book. Every single experience I have had with everyone at Hot Tree Publishing has been wonderful.

Now, let's talk about this beautiful cover. Thank you to Booksmith Cover Designs for another perfect fit for the series, the super fast work, and meticulous match to the first cover in the series.

Thank you to Allie for always being there to let me bounce ideas off of her, talk me through the lows and celebrate the highs.

To my husband and my sons, I love you and beyond appreciate the support you always have of my writing goals and dreams. Even if it means I occasionally forget to make dinner on time.

ABOUT THE AUTHOR

Science teacher by day, writer and baseball mom by night, Carolyn LaRoche lives near the ocean with her husband, two boys, rescue puppy, and four cats. She loves crocheting, books, food videos and trying new recipes.

Join my newsletter:

www.carolynlaroche.wordpress.com

I'd love to hear from you directly, too. Please feel free to email me at carolynlarocheauthor@yahoo.com or check out my website www.carolynlaroche.wordpress.com for updates.

- facebook.com/CarolynLaRocheAuthor
- twitter.com/CarolynLaRoche
- instagram.com/CarolynLaRocheAuthor
- bookbub.com/authors/carolyn-laroche
- goodreads.com/carolynlaroche

ALSO BY CAROLYN LAROCHE

If you loved *Murder on the Mountain*, you might enjoy the
other romantic and suspenseful stories and books
Carolyn LaRoche has published.

MARSHALL BROTHERS

Murder on the Mountain

Blue Ridge Murder

DEFENDERS OF LOVE

Witness Protection

Homeland Security

Border Patrol

ABOUT THE PUBLISHER

Hot Tree Publishing opened its doors in 2015 with an aspiration to bring quality fiction to the world of readers. With the initial focus on romance and a wide spread of romance subgenres, Hot Tree Publishing has since opened their first imprint, Tangled Tree Publishing, specializing in crime, mystery, suspense, and thriller.

Firmly seated in the industry as a leading editing provider to independent authors and small publishing houses, Hot Tree Publishing is the sister company to Hot Tree Editing, founded in 2012. Having established in-house editing and promotions, plus having a well-respected market presence, Hot Tree Publishing endeavors to be a leader in bringing quality stories to the world of readers.

Interested in discovering more amazing reads brought to you by Hot Tree Publishing? Head over to the website for information:

www.hottreepublishing.com

[f] facebook.com/hottreepublishing

[twitter bird] twitter.com/hottreepubs

9 781922 359421